A Highlander Christmas

Also by Janet Chapman

Moonlight Warrior
The Man Must Marry
Secrets of the Highlander
The Stranger in Her Bed
The Seduction of His Wife
Only with a Highlander
The Dangerous Protector
Tempting the Highlander
The Seductive Impostor
Wedding the Highlander
Loving the Highlander
Charming the Highlander

JANET CHAPMAN

A Highlander Christmas

POCKET **STAR** BOOKS

New York   London   Toronto   Sydney

Copyright © 2009 by Janet Chapman

POCKET STAR BOOKS and colophon are registered trademarks of Simon & Schuster, Inc.

Cover art by Alan Ayers
Cover design by Min Choi

Manufactured in the United States of America

ISBN-13: 978-1-61523-628-2

To those of you who don't believe in miracles, get ready, because you're going to get them anyway!

A Highlander Christmas

Chapter One

The only thing stopping Grey from strangling the shivering man crouched in front of their hearth was that he didn't wish to upset Grace. And since his wife already looked pale enough to pass out, Greylen MacKeage contented himself with glaring at his son-in-law and chief of police, Jack Stone, who had *brought* the half-frozen man to them.

Apparently also stunned by the news, Jack merely shrugged.

"Would you mind repeating what you just said, Mr. Pascal?" Grace whispered, clutching the arms of her chair. "As I don't believe I heard you correctly the first time."

Luke Pascal turned from warming his hands at the fire, his worried glance darting to Grey before returning to Grace. "When I went to NASA and asked to see her a couple of months ago, I was told that Camry hasn't worked there since December of last year. Then when I went to her condo, I found out she had sold it sometime last spring. I'm sorry I've obviously shocked you, Dr. Sutter, but I assumed you knew. "

Honest to God, if Pascal didn't stop calling his wife Dr. *Sutter,* Grey really was going to strangle the bastard. "And how is it that ye know our daughter?" he asked.

Luke Pascal stood up from his crouched position and faced Grey. "I've been communicating with Camry by e-mail for quite some time." He shifted uncomfortably. "Or I had been up until this summer, when she suddenly stopped e-mailing me back."

Grace suddenly jumped to her feet, which made Pascal step back. "*You're* the Frenchman who was giving Camry fits?"

Pascal's chill-drawn face flushed. "I prefer to think we were engaged in a lively scientific discussion. It certainly wasn't my intention to give her fits." He winced. "Though judging from some of her e-mails, I can see that I may have hit a nerve or two."

"And you say she stopped e-mailing you last summer?"

"Right after I suggested that I should come to America so we could collaborate."

"My daughter didn't think that was a good idea?" Grey asked, drawing Pascal's attention again.

The man took another step back. "According to her last e-mail, I would have to say no, she didn't."

"But you came anyway."

Their slowly thawing guest looked at Grace, obviously knowing she was the scientist in the family and apparently deciding he'd rather deal with her. "I am this close to finally unlocking the secret to ion propulsion," he said, holding his thumb and index finger an inch apart. "And I was sure that if Camry and I tackled the problem together, we could have a working prototype within a year."

"And her reply was?"

"A rather succinct no," he muttered, edging back toward the fire. His navy blue eyes moved from Grace to Grey. "You haven't spoken with her at all in the last year?"

Jack snorted, and Grey shot him a glare, which he then turned on Pascal. "Camry's been home several times, but she always led us to believe she was returning to Florida whenever she left."

"And since she has a cell phone," Grace interjected, "we never bother calling her lab." She collapsed back in her chair, shaking her head. "I just spoke with her a few days ago, and she told me her work was going great." She lifted distressed eyes to Grey. "Why didn't she tell us she'd left NASA? And if she sold her condo, where is she living now?"

Not wanting to discuss family matters in front of a stranger, Grey headed toward the foyer. "Come, Pascal. I'll take you to our resort hotel and get ye a room."

"No," Grace said, jumping to her feet again. "Luke will stay here at Gù Brath."

"That isn't necessary," Pascal said, correctly reading Grey's desire that he get the hell out of their house. "I really don't wish to intrude. If I can just sleep in a warm bed for a couple of days to thaw out," he said with an involuntary shiver, "and get some hot food in my stomach, I will be good to go. I really should be heading back to France anyway, before I find myself out of a job."

"But I thought you came here to collaborate with Camry?"

"But Camry doesn't wish to collaborate with me, Dr. Sutter."

Grace waved that away, then suddenly looped her arm through his, walking him past Grey toward the stairs leading to the bedrooms. "Please call me Grace, Luke. I haven't been called 'Doctor' in years. Where are your belongings?"

"In my rental car, buried under three feet of snow someplace out there," he said, motioning with his hand. "I had no idea Maine got such fierce blizzards this early in the season. I thought February and March were your snowy months. I must have walked ten miles before Chief Stone came cruising by on his snowmobile."

Grace stopped at the bottom of the stairs and turned to the men. "Jack, could you find Luke's car and get his belongings for him?"

Jack nodded. "Not a problem, Mother Mac."

She started walking up the stairs, Luke still in tow. "In the meantime, I'll find you something to wear, and while you're taking a warm shower, I'll throw together a nice hot meal for you."

They walked along the balcony, and Pascal gave one last wary glance toward the foyer before disappearing down the hall.

Grey turned to his son-in-law, but Jack raised his hand. "Give me two hours, and I'll be able to tell you everything you want to know about Luke Pascal, right down to his birth weight."

"And you'll find out where the hell Camry is."

"Well, that might be a little harder," Jack told him. "If Cam's been lying to us for over a year about where she's working and living, she's certainly smart enough not to leave a paper trail."

"I'll call her, and you can trace her cell phone signal."

Jack shook his head. "That would require involving the feds, and I doubt they'd consider a father searching for his grown daughter to be a threat to homeland security."

"Then use your own skills for tracking down runaways."

"It often took me months to find those kids, Grey, and then most times it was sheer luck. Maybe Winter or Matt could help. Or Robbie."

"No, I don't wish to involve anyone else in this. Camry's been lying to them as well, and I would rather find out her reason first, and not embarrass her in front of the entire family."

Jack nodded. "I can respect that. I'll quietly track her down, but it might take a while. And anyway, the solstice birthday bash is only a little over two weeks away. You can ask her what's going on then."

"She's not coming this year. She claimed she couldn't get away from work."

"I'm sorry. It's got to be hard finding out from a stranger that your daughter's been lying to you. But what I can't figure out is why." Jack chuckled softly. "Of all your girls, Cam would be the one to throw us a curve, but outright lying?" He shook his head. "That's the last thing I'd expect from her."

Grey glanced up at the balcony. "She's not the only one lying to us. About the only thing Pascal said that I believe is that the blizzard caught him by surprise. By the looks of his beard and the condition of his clothes, he's been camping out for a while. Where, exactly, did ye find him?"

Jack stepped over to the door and put his hand on the knob. "About twenty miles north of town, on one of the tote roads leading to Springy Mountain."

"And what excuse did he give for being out in the middle of nowhere?"

"He said he was looking for an old camp that his grandfather used to own. But the moment I introduced myself, he mentioned Camry's name. That's when I knew he'd been searching for whatever fell out of the sky and crashed north of here last summer." Jack glanced up at the empty balcony, then back at Grey. "Are you really going to let him stay in the house?"

Grey found his first smile of the afternoon. "Keep your friends close and your enemies even closer, Stone."

"And Pascal is the enemy?"

"Until he proves otherwise, he is."

*   *   *

Luke stood under the blessedly hot shower spray, gritting his teeth against the pain of his toes thawing, and began shaving off his beard with the razor he'd found in the fully supplied bathroom. As the evidence of his last two months of living like a caveman slowly fell away, he wondered if he hadn't just jumped out of the proverbial frying pan and into the fire.

First and probably most surprisingly, Grace Sutter MacKeage wasn't at all what he'd been expecting. For a woman with enough academic degrees—two of which were doctorates—to wallpaper a house, she sure as hell didn't appear to have one nerdy bone in her body. Luke knew she was in her mid-sixties and was the mother of seven girls, but she didn't look a day over fifty.

Her husband, however, sent chills through Luke that had absolutely nothing to do with his state of near frostbite. Greylen MacKeage had to be closer to seventy, and every damn year of experience showed in his sharp, piercing green eyes. When Luke had innocently mentioned that Camry hadn't worked for NASA for over a year, Greylen had appeared ready to kill the messenger—as if somehow it was *his* fault that Camry had been lying to them.

When Luke had found out his rescuer was

Jack Stone, who he knew was married to Camry's sister, Megan, he'd thought his luck had finally changed. That is, until he'd come face-to-face with the woman whose life's work he had destroyed. It had been all he could do not to throw himself at Dr. Sutter's feet and beg her forgiveness for destroying Podly.

Although to be fair, he'd only been trying to eavesdrop on Podly's transmissions, not hijack the little satellite. And he sure as hell hadn't meant to make it fall out of orbit. But to have it crash so close to Pine Creek . . . that was just outright eerie.

Then to have his childhood idol welcome him into her home and treat him with nothing but kindness? Well, he definitely was going to hell for his deceptions.

Luke turned to let the hot spray cascade over his clean-shaven face and started washing his hair. Stone hadn't believed him about searching for an old family camp; Luke had read the suspicion in the quiet lawman's eyes before he'd even finished telling the lie. So he'd switched to the half-truth that he knew Camry MacKeage, and that he thought she lived in Pine Creek. Chief Stone had then loaded Luke onto his snowmobile and driven the machine right through town, into the TarStone Mountain Ski Resort, and right up to what he could only describe as a castle. Hell, they'd even had to walk across a drawbridge to reach the front door!

So now what was he supposed to do? He'd just spent the last five months searching for Podly: the first three going over trajectory data, and the last two scouring Springy Mountain. And he still didn't have a clue where that satellite was; the damn thing could be at the bottom of Pine Lake for all he knew.

Once again, Luke fought the overwhelming urge to throw himself at Grace's feet, beg her forgiveness, then ask her to help him find *her* satellite that *he* had lost. But then all he had to do was picture Greylen MacKeage's piercing green eyes, and remember the lethal-looking antique sword he'd seen hanging over the hearth. Confessing might be good for his soul, but getting skewered by an enraged husband was another matter entirely.

Which brought Luke's thinking around to their daughter; did Camry take after her mother or her father?

Her father, he would guess, judging by some of her more scathing e-mails—which had actually fired his desire to meet her in person.

That is, until today. Now he wasn't so sure he wanted to lock himself in a lab with Camry, because if she had inherited any of her daddy's highlander genes, one of them might not come out alive.

Maybe *Grace* was the MacKeage he should be trying to collaborate with. He certainly wouldn't mind fulfilling his childhood dream of working with the legendary woman. It was Grace Sutter MacKeage, after all, who had turned him on to space travel when, at the age of twelve, he'd come across an article she'd written in a science journal, where she'd talked about her ongoing search for a more efficient rocket fuel.

But she was probably on the phone to her daughter right now, telling Camry about his unexpected and decidedly unceremonious arrival. And Camry was probably telling her mother to kick him out on his frozen ass.

How had his altruistic endeavor turned into such a fiasco?

All he'd been trying to do was unlock the secret to ion propulsion, but he'd ended up destroying the final piece of the puzzle instead. Did Grace even know her forty-year-long experiment was scattered over several square miles of densely forested mountain terrain?

She had to. The entire civilized world knew something had crashed in these mountains; he just didn't know if Grace was aware it was her beloved Podly.

Finally able to feel his toes again, Luke shut off the water and dried off. He wrapped the towel around his waist, padded into the large, tastefully decorated bedroom he'd been given, and stopped dead in his tracks.

While he'd been in the shower, someone had set clean clothes on the bed, started a roaring fire in the hearth, and placed a tray of food on a table in front of it.

Oh, yeah. He definitely was going to hell.

Chapter Two

"I really don't care what Jack found out about Lucian Pascal Renoir," Grace said, dropping her robe and stepping into the shower. She popped her head out to glare at Grey in the bathroom mirror. "I'm more concerned where Camry is."

"How in hell can ye have lived with me for thirty-five years and not learned some sense of security?" Grey said, his razor stopped halfway to his face. "Ye welcomed a complete stranger into our home, and even showed him your lab today."

Grace closed the shower curtain, lathered her sponge with lilac soap, and stepped under the spray. "I don't need a sense of security—I have you." She smiled when she heard him snort. "And if you could have seen Luke when I took him down to my lab this morning, you'd understand why I don't need to know everything about him," she continued. "The man actually kept his hands in his pockets, as if he were afraid to touch anything, and spoke in reverent whispers. It took me nearly an hour to persuade him that he could spend the afternoon down there by himself, and even catch up on his e-mail if he wanted."

The shower curtain suddenly opened, and her husband's face—half covered with shaving cream—popped into view. "Ye left a rival scientist in your lab all by himself all afternoon?" He sighed heavily. "That's what I mean, Grace. You're too damn trusting for your own good sometimes."

She pushed him out and slid the curtain shut. "You're letting in a draft. And Luke's not a rival scientist because I am not competing with anyone. We are all working toward the same goal of seeing mankind travel to other planets."

The shower curtain opened again and Grey stepped in, stole the sponge from her, and started lathering his broad chest. "The man has been all but stalking our little girl for a year, and ye gave him complete access to her work right along with yours."

Grace didn't have the heart to point out that he was going to smell like lilacs all day tomorrow.

"And as soon as you and Jack figure out where Camry is," she said, "I intend to send Luke after her."

Grey dropped the sponge in surprise. "You will not! Ye may have talked me into not calling her yesterday and demanding she tell us where she is, but when we do find her, I'll be going to get her, not Pascal. I don't trust the bastard. He's been lying to us since he got here. He didn't even tell us his real name."

Grace wrapped her arms around his neck and leaned into him. "He told us most of his name," she whispered, running a finger over his clenched jaw. "And he wasn't lying about Camry getting fired. I called her former boss this morning, and he told me he had been forced to let Camry go because she was so harried and unfocused, she was disrupting everyone else's work. I know you think you should be the one to go get her," she said in a rush, placing her finger over his lips when he tried to speak. "But think about it, Grey. If you drag Camry back to Gù Brath before she's ready to come home on her own, it will alienate her even more."

"Then what makes ye think Pascal can accomplish what I can't? Camry got so angry at the man that she stopped e-mailing him."

Grace bent down and picked up the sponge, turned her husband around, and started washing his back. "Exactly. Luke must have hit a power-fully raw nerve for her to walk away from the rousing argument they were having. Don't you remember what Camry was like last winter, Grey? She was so excited about her work and so angry at Luke, she could have flown to the moon under her own power. But then everything suddenly stopped last summer."

"Because Pascal said he was coming to America."

"Exactly. Coming face-to-face with someone she was that passionately involved with obviously scared the hell out of her."

He turned around to glare at her. "Camry fears nothing."

"No? Then why has she been lying to us for over a year? And why hasn't she been home since the summer solstice? Why won't she meet Luke in person? And why is she hiding from us, and from him, and from the work she loves?"

Grey leaned his forehead against hers and closed his eyes. "I don't know. I thought there wasn't any problem our daughters couldn't come to us with."

Grace wrapped her arms around his waist. "This isn't something you can fix, Grey. Camry has to fix herself." She smiled up at him. "And I hon-estly believe that Lucian Pascal Renoir is just the catalyst to get her roaring back into life again."

"Ye believe sending one liar after another will get us our little girl back?"

"No, I believe that two people, each of whom appears to be in desperate need of a miracle, can get themselves back. And I also believe that the next time we see our 'little girl,' she'll be a fully realized, self-empowered woman, and Luke Pascal will have that same dazed look on his face that all you men get when you suddenly realize you've met your match."

"And Camry is Pascal's match?"

"Aye, MacKeage," Grace said, mimicking his burr as she slid her hands up over his ribs. "I think those two lying young fools absolutely deserve each other. I need you tonight, husband," she whispered.

His arms around her tightened, and Grace felt the evidence of his own need pushing into her belly. He suddenly reached behind her and shut off the water, swept her up in his strong arms, and carried her into the bedroom.

"Do ye honestly believe that in all our years together, I haven't known what you're up to when you get all soft and pliable in my arms during one of our little discussions?" he asked, setting her down on the bed, then quickly covering her damp body with his.

She trailed a finger over his smile. "I prefer to

believe that I merely point out a reasonable course of action and, being the wise man that you are, you simply see things my way."

"And you've taught this trick to our daughters?"

"All seven of them," she said with a delighted laugh.

"May God have mercy on your soul, woman," he muttered, covering her mouth with his.

Grace looked up from the beautiful Christmas card she was holding and smiled at Grey sitting across the breakfast table. "You can tell Jack to stop searching for Camry," she said, pushing an envelope toward him. "Because we just found her."

Grey picked up the envelope, saw there wasn't a return address, and frowned.

"Read the postmark," she instructed.

"Go Back Cove, Maine?" He held out his hand to her. "Camry sent us a Christmas card?"

Grace handed him the card, which had an enchanting angel on the front, floating in a small forest clearing surrounded by fir trees dusted with snow. "Before you read the inside, take a moment to study the picture," she told him. "Besides the angel, what do you see?"

"I see a crow hiding in the trees," he said, his frown deepening.

Grace arched a brow. "Do we know any crows?"

His frown turned to an outright scowl, and he flipped open the card. "Your *unborn* great-grandson did not send us a Christmas card. See," he said, tapping the bottom of the card, "it's not signed *Tom,* it's signed only with an *F.*"

His frown returned. "What does this F person mean by thanking us for raising such a wonderful daughter?" He turned the card to see if there was anything written on the back, just as Grace had done earlier. Finding nothing, he reread the short note. "That's it? Just 'thank ye for raising such a wonderful daughter'? He or she doesn't even say *which* daughter." He tossed the card on the table between them. "It could be any one of our wonderful girls."

"F is referring to Camry," Grace insisted, picking up the card and smiling at the beautiful angel. She stood up and walked to the map of Maine hanging beside the back door over the row of coat pegs. "I've never heard of Go Back Cove, have you?"

Grey came over and also studied the map. "No. But *cove* implies water, so it must be on the coast."

"Or on any one of Maine's six thousand lakes and ponds." She went over to the computer on the counter next to the fridge, opened Google Earth, and typed in "Go Back Cove, Maine." "You're right, it is on the coast," she said, pointing at the map on the screen. "It's about thirty miles north of Portland."

Luke Pascal walked into the kitchen but stopped in the doorway when Grey turned and frowned at him. "Luke," Grace said, going over and holding out the card. "We found Camry. She's living in Go Back Cove, Maine." As soon as he took the card, she led him over to the computer. "It's a small town on the coast, north of Portland."

Luke moved his gaze from the computer screen to the open card in his hand, then turned it to see if there was anything written on the back. "Who is F?" he asked.

Grace waved his question away, rushing to the table to get the envelope. "We don't know, other than that it's obviously someone who knows Camry."

"But he or she doesn't even mention her by name," Luke said, taking the envelope and reading the postmark. He glanced uncertainly at Grey, then at Grace. "So how do you know it's Camry this F person is talking about?"

"Of course it is. All of our daughters are wonderful, but Camry's the only one who's missing right now."

"This handwriting looks feminine," he said, closing the card to study the angel on the front. He turned sympathetic eyes on Grace. "I realize it's distressing not knowing where Camry is, Dr. Sutt—I mean Grace," he quickly corrected, darting a frantic look at Grey.

Grace had finally had to explain to Luke that her husband preferred *MacKeage* to Sutter, before the younger scientist had finally started calling her by her first name.

"But what I don't understand," he continued, "is how you can conclude that a half-signed Christmas card, that doesn't even mention her name, tells you Camry is living in Go Back Cove."

"Do you believe in magic, Luke?" she asked, ignoring her husband's not-so-subtle growl.

"Magic?" Luke repeated with a frown.

"How about serendipitous coincidence, then?"

"Excuse me?"

Grace sighed and took the card and envelope from him. "Okay then, let's just call it *mother's intuition,* shall we?" She waved the card between Luke and Grey. "You will both simply have to trust me when I say that Camry is living in Go Back Cove." She looked at her watch, then at Luke. "It's only nine. If you leave right after lunch, you should be there in plenty of time to settle into your hotel."

"Excuse me?" he repeated, looking even more confused.

Grey sighed, only much more heavily than Grace had. "You're going to Go Back Cove, Pascal, to talk our daughter into coming home."

Luke's eyes widened and he took a step back. "I am?"

"But you only have two weeks to make it happen," Grace interjected. "We want her home by the winter solstice."

Luke took another step back, his alarm evident. "Considering Camry's last e-mail to me, I am probably the last person she wants to see. And this really is a family matter, don't you think? Shouldn't the two of you go after her?"

"We can't," Grace told him.

"But why?" he asked, tugging on the sleeve of his shirt.

"Because she can't know that we know she was fired from NASA, much less that we know she's been lying to us," Grace explained. "She has to *want* to come home, and she needs to tell us in person what she's been doing for the last year."

"Then how am I supposed to persuade her to come home if I can't reveal how worried you are about her?"

"That should be easy for you, Renoir," Grey said. "Ye just elaborate on the lies you've been telling *us*."

Luke dropped his gaze to Grace's feet, but then he suddenly stiffened, as if fighting some urge, and looked at Grey. "My full name is Lucian Pascal Renoir, but I go by Luke Pascal . . . sometimes." He tugged on his sleeve again, as if the borrowed shirt irritated him. "And because Camry knew me as Lucian Renoir from my e-mails, and I thought she might be here when Jack Stone found me, I told him my name was Pascal so I wouldn't get thrown back out in the snow on my as—on my ear."

"Then when you arrive in Go Back Cove," Grace said, pulling out a chair at the table and urging him to sit down, "I suggest you continue using 'Luke Pascal.' "

"But . . ."

She patted his shoulder. "It'll be okay, Luke," she assured him, going to the oven and getting the plate of eggs and toast she'd kept warming for him. "As soon as you're done with breakfast, you can sort through your belongings and give me what clothes need to be washed. Then we'll get on the Internet and find you a hotel in Go Back Cove. It's a small town, so it shouldn't take you too long to find Camry."

"My car was recovered?"

Grace set the plate down in front of him. "Jack and his deputy brought it back just this morning.

It's parked in the upper driveway behind the kitchen."

"Really, Dr. Sutter, I don't think I'm the one to go after your daughter."

"Of course you are, Luke. Because if I know Camry, the moment you work up the nerve to tell her that Podly is scattered over half of Springy Mountain, she'll drag you back here so fast your head will be spinning."

Luke snapped his navy blue eyes to hers, his face draining of color. "Y-you know about Podly?" he whispered, glancing at Grey before looking back at her. "You *know* it was your satellite that crashed here last summer?"

Grace went to the fridge to get him some juice, giving her equally stunned husband a smug smile as she walked by. "Do you honestly believe I wouldn't know someone was eavesdropping on Podly's transmissions?" she asked, bringing the juice back to Luke. "All the time you and Camry were burning up the Internet with your e-mails, I was watching you watching Podly."

"Did Camry know?" he asked, absently taking the juice she handed him.

"I never told her. But if she'd bothered to check, she's certainly smart enough to have found out. But then, I doubt she would have been looking for an eavesdropper."

"But you were?"

Grace shrugged. "An old habit from my days working for StarShip Spaceline."

He looked down at his plate. "Then you also know that I caused the satellite to malfunction." He looked up at her, his eyes filled with sincere remorse. "I'm sorry. I really don't know what I did to make it crash. I spent three months going over the data in my own lab, and the last two months scouring the mountain, hoping I could find enough salvageable parts to figure out what went wrong." He turned in his seat to face her fully and took her hand in both of his. "You have my word, Dr. Sutter, I was going to bring whatever I found directly to you. I-I'm sorry," he repeated.

Grace patted his shoulder. "I believe you, Luke." She nudged him around to his plate of rapidly cooling food. "Now eat, so we can get you packed up and headed to Go Back Cove. The sooner you find Camry, the sooner you can talk her into helping you find our satellite. Podly had heat shields in case something like this happened, so there's a good chance the data bank survived reentry. Camry knows these mountains quite well, and between your trajectory data and her love of a good challenge, I'm sure you'll both be locked in my lab with Podly by the winter solstice. Eat," she repeated, pointing at his food when he tried to say something else.

He snapped his mouth shut with a frown and picked up his fork.

Grace took hold of her also frowning husband and led him up the back stairway.

"That's it?" Grey asked as soon as they reached the upstairs hall. "The man destroys your life's work, and ye not only hand it over to him, you practically hand him our daughter as well?"

"Luke didn't destroy anything," she said, pulling him into their bedroom and closing the door.

"He just told ye he crashed Podly."

"No, he told me he *thinks* he caused Podly to crash." She stepped into his arms and started toying with one of the buttons on his shirt. "And I merely let him believe that he did," she said softly.

Grey's hands went to her shoulders. "Did *you* crash the satellite?"

"I was rather busy right about then, Grey. If you remember correctly, our baby girl was giving birth to our granddaughter at that precise moment."

"Then if you didn't make it crash, and Pascal didn't, who did?"

"I have no idea." She started toying with his buttons again, undoing the top one. "Maybe the same person who sent us that Christmas card?

Because what are the chances that my satellite would crash so close to my home?" She looked up. "The odds of that happening are astronomical, Grey. It *has* to be the magic."

He reached up and stilled her hand just as she undid the next button. "I find myself growing worried about ye, wife."

"How's that?" she asked, still managing to undo the next button.

"You've been acting far too much like *me* lately."

Grace went perfectly still. Oh God, he was right! She'd turned into a *warrior,* only instead of wielding a sword, her weapon was deceit.

She headed for the door. "I'm going to go tell Luke everything."

"Oh, no you're not," he said, sweeping her up in his arms with a laugh and striding to their bed. "If ye confess to Pascal, then *I'll* be forced to go get Camry, and I agree it would turn out badly for all of us."

He opened his arms and dropped her on their bed, then quickly settled on top of her. "I'm not upset ye guilted Pascal into going after Camry, only that I hadn't thought of it myself." He started undoing the buttons on her blouse. "But then, I didn't have all the pieces of the puzzle, did I? So when were ye going to tell me your little satellite is

scattered over half of Springy Mountain? I would
have found it for ye, Grace."

"I know you would have, and I love you for
that. But Podly really isn't mine anymore, Grey.
It's Camry's future. And I need for her to *want* to
go find it herself."

"And is the secret to ion propulsion sitting
under three feet of snow right now?"

"Yes."

He stopped undressing her. "Ye solved the
puzzle? Then we have to go get it!"

He started to get up, but Grace pulled him
back. "No, we don't. Podly's been holding the
secret for twenty years; I think it can wait another
couple of weeks."

"Twenty years! Ye solved the problem twenty
years ago, and you've been letting it orbit the
Earth all this time? Grace, that's been your life's
work!"

"Don't get so excited," she soothed, cupping
his cheeks and setting her thumbs over his lips.
"I didn't find the answer, *Camry* did—when she
was twelve."

He tried to sit up, but she held him over her.
"One day when Camry was twelve, she was down
in the lab with me, working on a project for her
school science fair. But then she started looking
over my shoulder and asking me one question

after another about what I was doing. And when I told her the particular problem I was having, she merely pointed at the screen and asked why I simply didn't transpose two seemingly disconnected integers in the equation I was working on."

She gently patted his cheeks when he frowned, and gave a soft laugh. "Don't ask me to explain it right now, or we'll still be in this bed come spring. Anyway, it might have been a question from an unschooled child, but it was pure genius. I reversed the numbers, which forced me to change several more, and within an hour I knew I could make ion propulsion work."

"And why didn't ye shout it to the world?"

"Because unlocking the code actually created a whole new set of problems. I couldn't really claim I had mastered ion propulsion, because I hadn't figured out how to actually *control* it." She sighed. "Ions can be used for more than just propulsion, Grey; they can also be used as a weapon. I wasn't ready to go there, because I wasn't sure the world was ready to go there."

"And now?" he asked. "If Camry and Pascal find Podly like ye hope, and they discover the secret, is the world ready now?"

"Don't you think I've been asking myself that question all this time?"

He reared up slightly. "So that's what you've

been doing for the last twenty years, when ye
locked yourself in your lab? Instead of trying to
figure out how to make ion propulsion viable,
you've been working on how you can keep it
from being used as a weapon?" He frowned again.
"Have ye succeeded?"

"Almost. But I'm sure that if Camry, Luke, and
I put our heads together, we can hand the world
a propulsion system that can be used for space
travel." She cupped his cheeks again. "And if
some other scientist takes our work and turns it
into a weapon . . . well, I've finally made peace
with the fact that all I can control is *my* contribu-
tion to mankind, which will be a more efficient
propulsion system."

"And if Pascal doesn't feel the same way?"

"Then he will have to live with his decision, as
every scientist must." She smiled. "But sometimes
we simply have to trust the magic, don't we, when
it starts messing with us? If you look at all the coincidences that brought Luke to our door, you have
to realize there's no such thing as a coincidence."

Grey groaned, laying his forehead on her. "If
you're trying to tell me that Winter or Matt had
anything to do with any of this, I swear I'll—"

Grace placed her finger over his mouth. "Not
them," she said with a laugh. "I believe it's someone even more magical."

"Who?"

"On the winter solstice, when my house is overflowing with *all* my children and grandchildren, then I will tell you who I think it is. Make love to me, husband. Take me traveling beyond the stars under *your* power."

Chapter Three

At about the same time a half-frozen Lucian Pascal Renoir was walking across the drawbridge of Gù Brath, Camry MacKeage was being dragged toward the beach of Go Back Cove by three massive dogs and one clueless dachshund that thought it was God's gift to the world. As soon as she saw that the beach was completely deserted— which wasn't surprising, considering it was only a few degrees above freezing—Camry unsnapped all four leashes and released her charges.

"Go on!" she shouted, racing after them with a laugh. "Run until you drop so we can get home and take a nap. I have to tend bar tonight!"

She ran along behind them for maybe a mile,

until a stitch in her side forced her to stop. It was as she was bent over with her hands on her knees, watching her panting breath condense in the cold air, that she heard what sounded like someone sobbing.

Camry straightened and looked around but saw only the dogs racing back toward her, their having discovered she was no longer following. She headed toward the dead grass and dormant rugosa rose bushes separating the beach from the old county road, her ear chocked in the direction the sound was coming from. She suddenly stopped at the sight of a girl, huddled shivering inside a totally inadequate jacket, her face buried in her knees.

"Hey, there," Cam said, slowly approaching.

The girl snapped her head up, her crystal blue eyes huge with surprise.

Cam stopped several yards away when the girl frantically looked around, as if searching for an escape route. "Hey, it's okay," she said gently, shoving her hands in her pockets. She shrugged, smiling at the girl. "I'm sorry if I startled you. I thought the beach was deserted."

The three large dogs descended on Camry, kicking up sand as they screeched to a halt and started wrestling with one another at her feet. The dachshund, its tongue whipping its cheek as it panted to catch up, suddenly changed direction.

"Tigger!" Camry cried just as the dachshund launched itself at the girl.

The previously sobbing young woman caught the small dog with a gasp, then gave a strangled giggle when Tigger started washing her face.

The three other dogs, suddenly realizing there was a new toy on their beach, took off. Camry lunged after them, but was able to grab only one by the collar. The other two plowed into the girl, sending her onto her back and forcing her to cover her face to protect herself from their slobbering tongues.

"Max! Ruffles! Get off her!" Cam shouted, her lone captive dragging her to the girl's rescue. She finally had to let go of the whining German shepherd in order to deal with the black Lab and golden retriever. She pushed the two larger dogs off the girl and scooped Tigger up in her arms, then had to use her knee to shove away the shepherd, who was determined to get in a few slobbers of its own.

Desperate to save the girl from getting licked to death, Camry set Tigger down, grabbed the hysterically giggling young woman, and hauled her to her feet. "Jeesh, I'm sorry," she said, trying to push away the excited dogs. "They won't hurt you, I promise."

The girl instantly sobered and blinked at her.

"They're really just four-legged cupcakes," Cam said, grabbing Max's collar when the Lab knocked the girl back a step. Cam shoved the dog away, then picked up a short piece of driftwood. "Fetch!" she shouted, flinging it toward the beach.

The three large dogs immediately shot after it, but Tigger sat down and started whining, staring up at the girl. The young woman picked up the dachshund and hugged it to her chest.

"I'm Camry. And that bundle of ecstasy you're holding is Tigger."

The girl said nothing, merely rubbed her cheek against Tigger's fur.

"Do you live around here?" Cam asked, scanning the road behind the low dunes for signs of a car—although she wasn't even sure the girl was old enough to drive.

"No," the girl whispered, her beautiful blue eyes wary.

"Do you have a name?"

"Fiona."

Cam didn't even try to hide her surprise. "Really? Fiona?" She smiled broadly. "I have a five-and-a-half-month-old niece named Fiona. Um . . . Fiona what?"

The girl didn't answer, but merely rubbed her cheek over Tigger's fur again.

Cam sighed. Judging by the condition of her clothes, and the fact that she was reluctant to give her full name, Camry figured the girl was a runaway. Another contributing factor was that Fiona looked as if she hadn't seen a bar of soap or hot water for a week, or a decent meal in days. She was pale and shivering, and looked so vulnerable, Cam just wanted to pull her into her arms and hug her senseless.

"If you don't live around here, then you must just be passing through. Do you have a place to stay tonight?"

"I was told there's a shelter down in Portland."

Camry fought to keep her horror from showing. Surely the girl wasn't hitchhiking! "Portland's thirty miles from here. I tell you what," she said, backing onto the beach. "I live close by, and have a spare bed at my place. And I have this really huge fireplace we could build a roaring fire in, and a hot-water supply that will let you take an hour-long shower if you want." She canted her head with a lopsided grin. "And it just so happens I was planning to drive into Portland tomorrow, so I could give you a ride."

That is, assuming she couldn't talk her into going home instead.

When she saw that Fiona was following—albeit hesitantly—Cam turned and slowly started walking up the beach toward her house. "I have to go to work tonight," she continued conversationally, "but the pub where I tend bar has some of the best food this side of Portland." She smiled over at Fiona, who had fallen into step beside her, still hugging Tigger tightly, apparently enjoying the warmth.

But then Fiona suddenly ran inland, and Cam's heart sank at the sight of the girl bolting, until she realized she was taking off with Tigger!

"Hey, my dog!" she shouted, giving chase.

Fiona just as suddenly stopped in the grass and set Tigger down, reached behind a bush, and straightened with a large backpack in her hand.

Cam sighed in relief. "Oh, good," she said, starting down the beach again as if nothing had happened. "I also have a washer and dryer, if you need to do laundry."

"What will your husband say about your letting me stay the night?" Fiona asked, rushing to catch up, the pack slung over her shoulders and Tigger back in her arms.

"I don't have a husband."

"Oh. You're divorced, then?"

Camry gave her a sidelong glance. "No. I've never been married."

Fiona stopped to blink at her. "How old are you?"

Camry blinked back. "Almost thirty-two. Why?"

"And you've *never* been married?"

She started walking again. "Last I knew, it wasn't a crime to be thirty-two and single. How about you? You married?"

"I'm only sixteen!"

Cam smiled. "I don't believe it's a crime to be single at sixteen, either. So Fiona, what's so exciting about staying in a shelter in Portland?"

The girl didn't answer for several heartbeats, then quietly said, "It's got to be better than living at home."

"I see. Pretty bad, is it?"

"My father is impossible. It seems as if every time I turn around, he's lecturing me about something."

Cam snorted. "Tell me about it. What is it between fathers and daughters, anyway? It's like the minute we're born, a man's lecturing gene kicks into high gear."

Fiona stopped again. "Your father lectured you, too?"

"Are you kidding? He's *still* lecturing me."

"At thirty-two?" She hugged Tigger closer. "Sometimes my dad treats me like I don't have the sense to come in out of the rain. He doesn't like most of my friends, especially the boys, and he doesn't like how I dress."

Camry grabbed the stick from the shepherd's mouth and threw it down the beach, sending the three dogs scurrying after it. She started walking again. "Oh, yeah? Just wait until you're two years out of college and still unmarried. Then the lectures change from warnings that 'all men are wolves,' to 'how come you can't find a man?' And by the time you're thirty, they change again to 'ye can't give me grandchildren if ye don't find yourself a husband,' " she said, mimicking her father's highland brogue.

Fiona giggled at the stern expression Camry gave along with the accent and covered her mouth with her hand. "Are you serious?" she asked, her big blue eyes widening. "The lectures are *never* going to stop?"

"Nope. And you know why?"

"Why?"

"Because we daughters scare the hell out of our daddies. They love us to death, and worry about us so much, that they can't stand our not having a husband to take care of us."

"We *scare* our fathers?" Fiona snorted. "I don't think anything scares my dad."

Camry saw the girl hug Tigger on a shiver, and started walking again. "*You* scare him, because he loves you. That's my house, right there," she said, pointing to the small cottage sitting on the bluff.

"Wow, you live right on the beach. Are you rich?"

Camry laughed. "Not exactly. I'm just renting. How about you? Are you rich?"

Fiona snorted. "Money isn't everything, you know."

"But it sure helps buy designer jeans, expensive backpacks, and fancy watches, doesn't it?" she said, nodding at the watch on the girl's wrist.

"I can't help it if my parents are rich," Fiona said defensively.

"No, just like you can't help that they're probably so worried right now, they've got every law enforcement official in the state looking for you. How long have you been on the run, Fiona?"

"Not long enough," she snapped, spinning around and heading for the house.

Cam gave a sharp whistle and the three dogs bounded up to her. "Come on, let's get the sand off you before your loving masters come pick you up," she told them, running to catch up with Fiona. "Hey, I wouldn't be a responsible adult if I didn't at least *try* to point out that your family is worried sick about you."

"They probably don't even realize I'm missing."

"Trust me, any father who loves you enough to lecture you definitely knows when you're not sleeping in your bed. I swear I couldn't sneak out of our house after dark without running into my father at the end of the driveway." She opened the door and motioned for Fiona to precede her onto the enclosed porch. "Don't let the dogs in the house. I have to wipe the sand off them first. Just set Tigger down and go warm up. I'll be right along."

"I'll help."

Camry handed her an old towel. "Okay. The Lab's name is Max, the golden is Ruffles, and the shepherd is Suki. I've got to get them spit-shined before their parents pick them up in an hour."

"They're not yours?"

"Good Lord, no. What would I want with this pack of overgrown babies? I just dog-sit them while their owners work to keep them in kibble. You know, sort of like a doggie day care."

"That's it? That's what you do for a living?"

"It pays the bills. And I also bartend at a pub Friday and Saturday nights."

Fiona gaped at her.

"What?"

"But you said you're almost *thirty-two*. How come you don't have a real career?"

"You mean like Suzy Homemaker or president of the United States? Or maybe a rocket scientist or something?"

The young woman flushed to the roots of her

dirty-blond hair. "I'm sorry. I didn't mean you had to be something as brilliant as a rocket scientist. It's just that . . . well, you seem so smart and everything." She motioned toward the dogs. "I mean, is this all you're going to do for the rest of your life, babysit other people's dogs and serve drinks on weekends?"

Camry grabbed Max and started brushing the sand off his legs. "Rocket science isn't all you think it's cracked up to be," she muttered. "You going to stand out here shivering all afternoon, or help me clean up these mutts?"

Camry spent the next two days trying to persuade Fiona to call her parents, all the while making sure she didn't *sound* like a parent for fear the girl would take off on her own again. But all her efforts got her was a roommate who suddenly didn't seem in any hurry to leave.

She'd been stunned speechless the first night, when Fiona had emerged from the shower wearing the clothes she'd lent her. The girl was breathtakingly beautiful; her wavy, waist-length hair was actually strawberry blonde, her complexion was flawless, and in clothes that fit her far better than they did Cam, her figure would have made a dead man sit up and take notice.

Hell, if she was Fiona's daddy, she wouldn't

waste her time lecturing the girl, she'd lock her in her room until she was thirty!

She'd had second thoughts about taking Fiona to the Go Back Grill that first night, but since she had only three eggs and some outdated mayonnaise in the fridge, Cam had been forced to take her to work. So she'd sat the girl at the end of the bar to keep an eye on her, then stuffed her full of greasy, fattening food.

By the second night, she'd talked Dave Bean—who owned the Go Back Grill—into letting Fiona bus a few tables to pay for all the greasy, fattening food she'd been wolfing down as if she had a hollow leg.

But it was Sunday afternoon, and Camry was feeling more like a worried parent than a roommate as Fiona got ready for work. That's why she had Dave on the phone, giving him hell for giving the girl a permanent job!

"You can't have a sixteen-year-old on staff at a bar, Dave," Cam growled into her cell phone. "Child Services is going to come after you for hiring a minor."

"That's not what you said last night, when you kindly pointed out that her busing tables was perfectly legal," Dave growled back. "Make up your mind, Cam."

"It's only legal when *I'm* working there. Hey,

wait. If you hired her, what name did she put on the W-2 form?"

"Fiona Smith."

Camry snorted. "She had to give you a Social Security number. What is it?"

"Now, Cam, you know I can't give that out to anyone."

Camry looked around to make sure Fiona was still in the spare bedroom getting dressed, and turned her back and lowered her voice. "But she's a runaway, Dave. I called the police Friday, but they don't have any missing teens fitting her description. I need that number to find out who she really is so I can call her parents."

A heavy sigh came over the phone. "I know. But you're putting me between a rock and a hard place here. I promise, first thing tomorrow morning I'll turn Fiona's W-2 over to my accountant and ask him look into it. But it's probably a bogus number, just like Smith is obviously fake."

"Yet you hired her anyway."

"Because I'm desperate to find bus staff. Kids today don't want to work for an honest wage; they want Mommy and Daddy to just hand them money. And besides," he said, lowering his own voice. "I didn't dare say no when she asked me for a job, because like you, I want her hanging around long enough for us to find her parents."

Cam sighed in defeat. "At least it'll buy us time. But how am I supposed to keep an eye on her when I'm not scheduled to work? She'll be running around your bar, being watched by every single *and* married male in the joint."

"It's Sunday night, and I have nearly every table reserved up until nine," Dave countered. "And you know why? Because all the flyers I've been passing out have let everyone know that I've classed the place up and hired new staff."

"Then I want to come to work tonight, too."

"Betty's covering the bar tonight."

"Then I'll wait tables."

"I'm still recovering from the last time you waited tables. You're a good bartender, MacKeage, but you suck as a waitress."

"I promise, I won't dump anything on anyone."

A pained sigh came over the phone. "I'll keep an eye on your kid. She's just busing tables."

"She can bus on Fridays and Saturdays."

"But I've never had more than two reservations on a Sunday night."

"Which must mean you need extra staff."

He sighed again. "You promise you won't get smart-mouthed with my patrons, or dump any food on them?"

"Scout's honor."

"And you'll wear one of my new waitress uniforms?"

"Those . . . *things* hanging in the back room are uniforms?" She snorted. "I thought you wanted to turn the place into a *family* pub, not some pseudo-colonial bar with waitresses dressed like wenches. "

"Go Back Cove was supposed to have been a hideout for pirates back in the 1800s, and I'm simply playing up the old legend. I spent all last night and this morning redecorating the place."

"Fiona is *not* wearing a low-cut blouse and one of those leather bustier thingies. I swear I'll call Child Services myself if you put her in one of those sexist costumes."

"I have mostly bus *boys*, Cam. Fiona can wear jeans and a T-shirt, just like they do. But," he said before she could say anything, "you can wait tables tonight if you're willing to wear the new uniform."

Dammit, dammit, dammit. She didn't want to dress up like a wench!

Then again, she didn't want Fiona going to work without her, either.

But if she tried to talk the girl out of going to her new job, that made her no better than Fiona's parents. And she'd be damned if she was going to mother the child.

"What'll it be, Cam? You coming to work or not?"

"I'll be there," she snapped, hitting the End button when she heard Dave chuckle and slinging the phone at the couch.

"Are you going to stay and have supper when you drive me in?" Fiona asked, walking into the room. "Because there's still nothing in the fridge."

Camry closed her eyes and counted to ten, suddenly having a whole new appreciation for her own mother, who had managed to raise seven girls without losing her sanity. She opened her eyes, and, yup, her roommate was still dressed like a prostitute. "Um . . . is that one of the outfits your father objected to?"

Fiona looked down at herself, then smiled at Cam. "Yeah. He asked me if I'd stolen it off some hooker the last time he took me to New York City."

"Well . . . at the risk of sounding like your father," Camry said with a crooked grin, choosing her words carefully, "is there any chance I could get you to wear an oversize T-shirt and a pair of *my* jeans tonight?"

Camry held up her hand to forestall the objection forming on Fiona's lips, took a deep breath, and jumped right into the quagmire. "It's not that I don't think that's a fabulous outfit, but you're working in a *bar,* Fiona. And you're certainly old enough to realize that some men, when they've had a little more beer than they should, forget this is the twenty-first century and that women were not put on this Earth merely for their entertainment." She shrugged. "I know it's archaic, but I also know that you're bright enough to realize that sometimes we women are better off downplaying our assets instead of . . . accentuating them."

Oh God, those words could have come straight out of *her* mother's mouth!

Fiona stared at her for the longest time, saying nothing, then suddenly smiled. "Okay," she said, spinning around and heading back into the bedroom. "Can I wear your black jeans?"

"Yeah, go ahead," Cam said, closing her eyes in relief, suddenly remembering why the mere thought of having kids scared the hell out of her.

Chapter Four

Luke slid into the booth at the Go Back Grill, the smell of greasy food all but making him salivate. Though he was still trying to recover from two months of living on nothing but trail mix and rehydrated soup, he had to admit the results felt pretty damn good.

When he'd seen himself naked in the bathroom mirror at Gù Brath that first night, he'd been stunned to realize that he'd lost over twenty-five pounds of fat. But he'd probably added ten pounds of lean, hard muscle, and for the first time in years, Luke was more than casually aware of the six-foot-two, broad-shouldered body that housed his brain. He really had been spending too much time in the lab, and once he got back to work, he'd have to remind himself to get more exercise.

"Beer?" the waitress asked just as he opened the menu.

"What do you have for imported wine?" he asked absently, scanning the various food offerings that were thoughtfully accompanied by pictures.

"Red, white, or blush."

"What do you have for imported red?"

"That's it. Red house wine, white house wine, or blush," she said dryly. "You want anything fancier, you have to drive to Portland. We serve forty-two different beers, mixed drinks, and house wines."

Luke finally looked up with a frown, only to come face to . . . chest with a set of creamy white breasts being pushed out of an indecently low-cut blouse by an impossibly tight black leather corset.

The woman belonging to the breasts lifted his chin with the end of her pencil, forcing his gaze up to her scowling face. "Red, white, or blush," she repeated through gritted teeth.

"I'll have a Guinness," he said, carefully lifting his chin off her pencil and looking back at his menu. "And your largest steak, a baked potato—loaded—and coleslaw. *And,*" he said a bit more forcefully when she started to leave, "a large salad, no onions, with blue cheese dressing."

As she stomped away, Luke heard a soft giggle over the din of patrons. The young woman clearing the table across the aisle continued to laugh behind her hand as she watched his waitress leaving, then looked back at him.

Luke glanced around to make sure he was the one causing her amusement, then smiled at her. "Do you think I should give her a bigger tip for that stunt, or not leave her anything?" he asked.

The young girl tossed her rag in the bucket on her cart of dirty dishes, and walked over. "It took an act of Congress to get her into that uniform tonight," she said. "Add to that how uncomfortable that leather bustier is, and you're lucky she only used that pencil to close your mouth, instead of using it to poke out your eyes." She suddenly held out her hand. "Hello, I'm Fiona."

Surprised but utterly charmed by the beautiful young woman's straightforwardness, Luke took her offered hand and gently shook it. "Luke Pascal."

"Do you live here in Go Back Cove, Luke?" she asked. "Or are you just passing through?"

"I checked into the hotel across the street just a few minutes ago, but I plan to hang around awhile. I'm on sabbatical from work, and I thought I'd spend some time at the coast while I'm visiting Maine."

"The winter ocean is so desolate and lonely-looking, don't you think?" she asked. "Sometimes it's just a bleak gray that softly ebbs and flows, as if it were waiting for its true love to appear, and sometimes it's churning and angry, mad because that love is taking so long to show up," she said dreamily, her sad smile and crystalline blue eyes making her face practically glow.

Luke decided she wasn't charming, she was enchanting. She was beautiful, poised, and well spoken, and she reminded him of his baby half sister, Kate, who had a dramatic streak a mile wide and a romantic imagination to go with it.

"Table three needs clearing," his waitress told Fiona as she thunked Luke's bottle of Guinness—and no glass—down on the table without even looking at him. "If you don't want to get fired your first night, you better keep moving."

Completely unruffled by the waitress's stern handling, Fiona reached in her apron pocket and handed her some money. "Here. This is from table three."

"A buck?" the waitress growled, staring at the single dollar bill in her hand.

Fiona softly snorted. "I saw the man leave you a

ten, but when he went to pay the bill, the woman with him stuffed it in her purse and replaced it with a one."

The waitress turned her back on Luke to whisper to the girl. "I told Dave these stupid costumes would backfire on us. Go on, you better get hustling." She started walking away with her, still whispering. "You have to stop fraternizing with the customers, Fiona. This is a pub, not a social club."

"I'm sorry, Camry. I keep forgetting because I like meeting new people."

Luke didn't hear any more of their conversation as they moved away, but he did turn to stare after them.

Camry? As in Camry MacKeage? What in hell was a physicist doing working in a bar, dressed like an eighteenth-century wench?

Naw, it couldn't be her. The probability of stumbling across Dr. MacKeage after being in town less than an hour had to be a million to one.

Not that Go Back Cove was a thriving metropolis or anything. And *Fiona* could even be the F person who had sent the Christmas card.

What had Grace called it? Magic? Serendipitous coincidence?

Luke picked up his beer and took a long

swallow. Naw. He didn't believe in anything but cold hard facts, and then only if he could back them up with numbers.

Still, if he found out Miss Congeniality had piercing green eyes—assuming he could keep his gaze on her face long enough to find out—then the numbers had just turned a bit more in his favor, hadn't they?

"Here," Camry snapped, slapping the dollar bill on the counter in front of Dave. "Put this toward the damages."

"What damages?" her boss asked, frantically looking around.

"The damages I'm going to cause the next time one of your precious patrons stiffs me. I swear if I'd seen that woman swap my tip, I'd have chased her right out the door and stuffed that stupid dollar bill down her throat." She tugged on the bustier, which wasn't only cutting into her boobs but cutting off her breath, and glowered at Dave. "I told you these stupid uniforms would back-fire on us. The men are leaving us nice tips, but the women with them are scoffing them up as soon as the men turn their backs. For someone who claims he's trying to run a family pub, you seem to be moving in exactly the opposite direc-tion. Women patrons do *not* like being served by wenches with escaping anatomy, and mothers do *not* like their children staring up their waitress's skirt."

Dave sighed. "Doris told me she had a similar problem with the tipping, but she also said that the unaccompanied males are leaving double what they usually do." He grinned, shoving the dollar bill back across the counter. "So that evens things out."

"I've nearly dropped three trays of food because of these stupid heels," she muttered, shifting her weight to give her left foot a rest. "It has to be against insurance codes or something for wait-resses to serve in heels. If we don't kill someone with a falling tray, at the very least we could pop a tendon."

"It's not like they're stilettos or anything; they're only two inches high."

"Doris is nearly sixty, Dave. She's *limping*."

He sighed again. "I already told her to change back into her sneakers, even if they do look silly."

"You mean sillier than a grandmother show-ing enough cleavage to make a saint drool and enough leg to make a thoroughbred envious?"

He held up his hand. "Okay. Okay. The heels were a bad idea, and maybe the skirts are a bit short." He shrugged. "But hey, the rest of my new theme seems to be a hit. The kids really like the eye patches and swords I've been handing out, and I think we burned up a blender tonight making Jolly Roger Zingers."

He leaned over the counter toward her. "And I saw you prodding Fiona along a couple of times when she got chatty with the customers. Don't. They like talking to her, and she's giving the place a homey, friendly feel."

"Did you also see that guy try to slip a twenty-dollar bill in her apron pocket?"

Dave straightened with a frown. "I thought she handled that quite well. Unlike your little stunt last month, she didn't *accidentally* dump his drink over his head. She merely waggled her finger at him and scampered away."

"My guy wasn't trying to stuff money in my *apron*."

Dave sighed louder and harder. "Tell me again why you work here?"

Camry tapped her chin with her finger. "Gee, let me think. Maybe because on Columbus Day they rolled up the sidewalks and closed the town when the tourists left?"

"Portland's just down the road."

"I prefer the peace and quiet of this place."

"That's right, *Dr.* MacKeage, I forgot you came here from Florida." He snorted. "The problem with you brainy types is that you think we working stiffs don't know how to run our own businesses."

Camry gaped at him. "I am not an academic snob. The only reason you even know I hold a doctorate is because your stupid employment application asked me to list all my schooling."

"To which you had to add an entire page for all your degrees." He suddenly stared over her shoulder for several seconds, then glanced down the bar. "Betty," he said, motioning the bartender closer. "No more drinks for booth nine, okay? All four of those guys have had enough. And if they give Wanda any trouble, you have her come see me and I'll handle them."

"Okay, Dave," Betty said, returning to the blender she'd left running.

"And your point is?" Cam asked Dave the minute she had his attention again.

"What were we talking about?"

"I believe you had just implied I'm a snob."

"Oh, come on, MacKeage," he said with a sudden smile. "You need to lighten up. It doesn't look good in front of the staff when you give the boss grief. And I don't want to have to fire you, because"—he leaned closer—"I actually like you," he whispered, his smile widening as he straightened back up. "You sort of remind me of a Jack Russell terrier I used to have that was always growling at me, as if she needed a good fight to keep herself entertained."

"I remind you of your *dog*?"

"I loved that dog, God rest Pip's soul," he said with a laugh. He arched his bushy eyebrows at her. "You want to know what finally settled her down?"

"Not really."

"I got her a boyfriend, which in turn got her a litter of babies. Mellowed my little darling right out, those pups did."

Cam just gaped at him.

"So the moral of this little story," he had the audacity to continue, "is that instead of scowling at your customers, maybe you should trying smiling at them."

She snapped her mouth shut and scowled at *him*.

He sighed. "You've been living in Go Back Cove and eating here for what . . . seven or eight months? And working for me for two? And in all that time, I have never once seen you with a date."

"Maybe I'm gay," she snapped.

Dave chuckled. "Nope. It's not the girls I see you watching, it's the men. Oh, you're interested, all right. You're just too scared to actually play with the big boys."

Camry made a point of visually searching the wall behind the counter, even going on tiptoe to look down the length of the back wall of the bar.

"What are you looking for?"

"Your degree in psychology."

His laughter came straight from the belly as he took the slip and money from a customer who'd walked up to pay his bill. "My degree is from the school of hard knocks, kiddo, and it took me thirty years of tending bar to earn it." He hit some buttons on the register, then shot her a wink. "You watch Fiona working the room tonight, Cam, and maybe you'll learn something. That girl's got a gift for making people smile. How was your dining experience?" he asked the man, handing him his change.

"Delightful," the customer said, glancing over at Camry—specifically at her chest. "I've heard the food here is good, but I especially like the uniforms." He cleared his throat. "Except maybe they don't work so well on all your waitresses." He leaned closer to Dave and lowered his voice so Camry wouldn't hear.

But of course she did.

"That older waitress," he continued in a whisper. "I kept expecting the laces on her corset to pop and maim someone, and she tripped and nearly spilled beer on me."

"We're rethinking the uniforms."

"Or you could just hire younger waitresses," the lech suggested.

"Doris is the prettiest woman here," Camry growled at him. "And the best damn waitress we have!"

The man stepped away in alarm, and all but ran for the door.

Dave sighed again. "Will you lighten up?"

"Will you get real?" she said, spinning away and heading for the kitchen.

Honest to God, she really didn't know why she worked here.

Other than that it might be entertaining.

And she was *not* like some stupid old Jack Russell terrier!

She was a *happy* person, dammit, right down to her blistered toes.

Chapter Five

"Good Lord, what's wrong?" Fiona asked, pushing her busing cart into the kitchen and stopping beside Camry.

"What? Nothing. Why?"

"Because you look like you want to punch someone."

Camry took a deep breath—at least as deep as her stupid corset would allow—and forcibly shook off her foul mood. "Sorry. I was just wondering why I work here."

"Because you love people."

"I do?"

"Of course you do, silly," Fiona said with a laugh, giving her a playful punch on the arm.

"You spend all week with a bunch of dogs, so you need to work here on the weekends to remind yourself that you're human."

"My dogs are better behaved than some of the customers."

"You'd be bored to tears if you spent all your time around well-behaved people. That's what I like best about you, Cam. You say what you think, and you back up what you say with action."

"I do?"

"Sure. Take me, for instance. I know you've been wanting to browbeat my name out of me so you can call my parents, but you've been treating me like an adult even though I'm not one. That's why you can't bring yourself to go through my backpack to find my ID."

"How do you know I haven't?"

"Because I'm still here, aren't I? And you know why? Because I remind you of *yourself* when you were my age, and that's why you're so determined that I'll call my parents on my own."

Camry shot her a lopsided grin. "Did you say you were sixteen, or sixty?"

"MacKeage! Your order for table ten is getting cold," the cook shouted from the serving station. "Where in hell's your pager? I've been beeping you for ten minutes."

Cam felt at the back of her waist. "Damn, it

must have fallen off. It's probably kicking around under some table," she muttered, heading to the heat lamps to pick up her order. "Or more likely in some four-year-old's pocket."

"I'll help you look for it," Fiona said, abandoning her cart to follow her into the dining room. "I'll start searching the floor while you take Luke his food."

"Luke?" Cam repeated, weaving her way through the crowded pub.

"The big dreamy guy at table ten," Fiona explained, stepping around her to run interference when a young child bolted past them, waving a plastic sword and wearing an eye patch. She redirected the toddler back to his parents, then looked at Cam. "You don't think he's dreamy? His eyes are a really deep navy blue, and his hair's almost long enough to tie back. I love long hair on a man, don't you?"

Cam glanced toward table ten. "He's old enough to be your father."

The girl made an exasperated sound. "I don't think he's dreamy for *me*, silly, I think he's perfect for *you*. But he's only going to be in town a short while because he's on sabbatical, so you need to work fast. You should give him your phone number when you bring him his bill."

Camry nearly dropped the heavy tray she was holding. "What?"

Apparently thinking that was a rhetorical question, Fiona started running interference again, occasionally bending over to search under the tables. Deciding she better have a talk with her roommate on their ride home from work, Cam followed her toward the sidewall of booths. But just as Fiona walked past table ten, a hand suddenly snaked out from table nine, grabbed the young girl's arm, and pulled her into the booth of drunken men.

Fiona's yelp of surprise was also laced with pain when she hit the corner of the table. Without skipping a beat, Cam rushed forward with every intention of cleaning the jerk's clock. Only it was at that exact moment that table ten's Dream Guy shot out of his own booth and also launched himself at the jerk—his shoulder knocking the tray full of food out of Camry's hands and sending it crashing to the floor.

Pandemonium ensued when two of the jerk's drunken buddies scrambled out to go after Dream Guy at the same time that Camry also headed into the fray. Only her damn heels got tangled up in the broken dishes and food, and she ended up *falling* into the fight instead.

Her head exploded in pain when her cheek slammed into one man's elbow, which was cocked back to take a swing at Dream Guy. The force of the backward punch threw her into a nearby table, scattering dishes and food over people trying to scramble out of the way.

Camry straightened and spun around, frantically searching for Fiona in the tangle of bodies. She spotted the girl preparing to drive a fork into the arm of the jerk who was trying to pull her out from under the table by her hair. Cam screamed the girl's name at the top of her lungs, hoping Fiona could hear her over the sound of crashing dishes and the growls and grunts of the fighting men.

But it was too late. Even though Fiona tried to halt her downward swing as her eyes snapped to Camry, the fork still found its target. The ensuing shout of pain came just as another one of the drunken men flew backward, sending Camry to the floor with her own cry of pain as her ankle twisted under the weight of his landing on top of her.

Almost as quickly as it had begun, the pandemonium ceased when Dave, along with several of the grill's regular male patrons, started grabbing men by the scruffs of their necks and pulling them off Dream Guy and Camry.

Fiona immediately crawled over and lifted Cam into a sitting position, wrapping her arms around her protectively. Cam snatched the fork out of her fist just as Dave came over and crouched down in front of them.

"Damn, are you girls okay?" he asked, brushing hair back off Camry's face.

Cam jerked away when his fingers touched her throbbing cheek. "I just want to sit here a minute, okay?" she said shakily, carefully straightening her right leg.

"I've been stabbed!" a man shouted. "I'm bleeding! That bitch stabbed me!"

Dave looked down at the fork in her hand, which Camry immediately tossed under a nearby table. "You stay put until the ambulance gets here," he said, getting to his feet and going over to the loudly complaining victim.

Fiona knelt behind Camry and pulled her against her for support. "Other than that shiner that's already starting to swell," Fiona said, "what else hurts?"

"My ankle is throbbing like hell," Camry whispered. She turned to look up at Fiona. "Mind telling me what possessed you to stab that guy with a fork? You don't think that was a little . . . extreme?"

Fiona shrugged. "My dad always told me that if I'm ever accosted, I'm supposed to see everything as a weapon, and not hesitate to use it."

"Your father actually said that?"

She nodded soberly. "He said that I better not think like a woman, but like a warrior." She suddenly smiled. "And that a woman's greatest weapon is surprise, because men don't expect us to fight back."

Camry blinked up at her. "Your dad and my dad must have read the same book on raising daughters. Oh, God, I can't breathe," she groaned, twisting to face forward, trying to get air in her lungs as she frantically tugged on the laces of her bustier. "Help me get this stupid thing off."

Fiona tried to untie the lacing on the front but couldn't work the knotted bow free. "Luke," she cried as he sat down next to them, holding a napkin up to his temple. "Help me. Camry can't breathe."

"Cut this damn thing off," Cam panted, trying to find a position that allowed her to breathe. "Ow! My ankle!"

"Stop thrashing around. You're making it worse," Luke said. He dropped the napkin so he could hold her down, then unsnapped a pouch on his belt with his other hand. He pulled out a multitool and opened it to expose the blade. "Help me, Fiona," he instructed, tugging on the knotted bow. "Hold her chest out of the way."

Camry covered her own breasts. "You can't see what you're doing with blood in your eye," she said, worried he might cut more than just the laces.

While she covered her precious anatomy with her hands, Fiona used her own hands to block Cam's view of what he was doing. "He won't cut you, I promise," the girl said with all the bravado of someone whose boobs weren't inches from a sharp blade.

Camry felt several tugs on her torso, a very welcome release of pressure, and all of a sudden she could breathe again! She tried to roll to her side, but discovered that Luke was straddling her hips. His weight suddenly disappeared, but instead of standing up, he rolled to lie flat on the floor beside her.

"Slow down your breathing or you'll hyperventilate," he instructed, also taking labored breaths. "Damn, I think I have a couple of cracked ribs."

Fiona lifted Camry into a sitting position again, wedging herself behind her for support as Luke rolled toward her with a groan, then rose to his knees.

"Where else are you hurt?" he asked.

"She twisted her ankle," Fiona answered for her.

Luke sidled down to her legs and very gently slid her shoe off her right foot. It was as he went to look up at her that his gaze suddenly stopped, and Camry realized he could look right down her unconfined blouse! But when she slapped her hand to her chest and his gaze lowered, she realized he could also look right up her skirt! She started wiggling as she tugged on the hem, trying to pull her skirt down as she also tried to hold up the front of her blouse.

"What *is* your problem?" he snapped, falling back when her flailing left foot kicked his thigh— apparently quite close to his groin.

"Nothing!"

"I'm pressing charges against whoever stabbed me," Fiona's victim cried from three tables down.

Still holding her blouse to her chest, Camry dropped her head to her knees with a groan. "Honest to God, I am *never* stepping foot in another bar," she muttered, remembering the last time someone had wanted to press charges against her, after a barroom brawl in Pine Creek last summer.

Fiona patted her back. "I'll tell Dave I was the one who stabbed that jerk."

Camry straightened. "You will not. If the authorities find out your age, then *Dave* will get in trouble." She suddenly smiled. "Unless you want your parents to get a call from the police, telling them their missing daughter is sitting in jail. Just think of the lecture dear old Daddy's going to give you then. You won't see daylight for years."

"What do you mean, *missing daughter*?" Luke asked, his gaze darting between Cam and Fiona. He finally settled on Fiona. "Did you run away from home or something?"

"Or something," Fiona said.

Luke's gaze snapped to Camry. "You *know* she's a runaway, and you haven't done anything about it?"

"I suppose I could have left her on the beach. Or let her hitchhike to Portland so she could stay at a homeless shelter."

Luke reached in his pocket, pulled out his cell phone, and handed it to Fiona. "You have to call your parents right this minute, young lady. They must be worried sick about you!"

Camry couldn't believe how dense the guy was.

But even more, she couldn't believe that Fiona actually took the phone, flipped it open, and started pushing buttons.

Her mouth gaping in shock, Cam blinked at Luke.

He shot her a smug smile. "Apparently she responds to *male* authority."

Fiona suddenly handed the phone back to Luke.

"You didn't call them!"

"I will. Eventually." She gave him an equally

smug smile. "But I did add Camry's number to your phone list. Just in case you want to call her, seeing as how you're going to be here for a while and don't know anyone."

Luke looked down at his phone. He started pushing buttons with his thumb, his eyes suddenly widened, and he snapped his gaze back to Camry.

Cam held out her hand. "Give me that."

He flipped the phone closed and shoved it in his pocket.

"I'm changing my number first thing tomorrow."

"Okay, the cops and the ambulance are here," Dave said, walking over. "Folks," he said to the dining room of stunned patrons. "I'm sorry for the disturbance. If you stop at the counter on your way out, my staff will give you vouchers for a free meal. First, though, I believe the police wish to speak with each of you before you leave. You all come visit the Go Back Grill again, okay? And bring your friends!"

He crouched down in front of Camry. "Christ, Cam, that's one hell of a shiner you got there." He scowled at her ankle. "And you need to get that foot X-rayed. The ambulance will take you in, and you just tell them to bill me."

"All I need is an ice pack, because it's only

sprained. And I am not riding in an ambulance. They're for people having heart attacks or bleeding to death."

His scowl darkened. "Don't make me use my boss voice," he said, dismissing her by turning to Luke and holding out his hand. "Dave Bean, Mr. . . . ?"

"Pascal," Luke said, taking his hand. "Luke Pascal."

"I'm sorry, Luke, that you got caught up in this mess. But I did see you come to our little girl's rescue," he said, nodding toward Fiona, "and I thank you. Most people aren't so quick to get involved in other people's business."

Luke shrugged. "I have a kid sister about the same age as Fiona."

"Food's on the house for as long as you're in town, Luke." Dave looked at Luke's bleeding cut, and the way he was cradling his ribs. "You go with Cam in the ambulance and let them check you out at the hospital. That cut might need stitches, and you might have some cracked ribs. I'll cover the medical bills."

He turned back to Camry. "You did good, kiddo. Don't worry about anyone pressing any charges. By the time I'm done with those four, they'll wish they'd driven straight through town." He flushed and awkwardly patted her shoulder.

"You take as much time off as you need to get back on your feet. You want me to call anyone? Your family, maybe?"

"No!" Camry said a bit more emphatically than she'd meant to, causing Dave to flinch. "I mean, thanks, but I'm really not hurt that badly." She smiled over at Fiona. "And I happen to have a roommate at the moment, who can wait on me hand and foot for a few days."

Two EMTs came over, wheeling a gurney. One of the men crouched down in front of Luke and pointed a tiny flashlight in his eyes. The other one did the same to Camry. He must have decided she was going to live, because he grinned at her. "Can you hop up on the gurney yourself, or are you willing to risk being dropped if I go weak in the knees when I pick you up?"

"I want to change into my jeans and sweater before I go anywhere."

"Why? They're just going to take everything back off you at the hospital." He scanned his gaze over her costume, then grinned at her again. "What you're wearing is just lovely. And anyway, Doc Griswell's working the ER tonight, and he's got a thing for legs—I mean ankles. I bet he puts you ahead of the stab wound and facial cut."

Camry made an effort to stand, but the ruggedly built EMT suddenly lifted her in his arms, stood up, and set her on the gurney. "It's a good thing you didn't crack a smile," he said dryly, spreading a blanket over her, "or I really would have gone weak in the knees."

"Fiona, why don't you go get Camry's purse and clothes," Luke suggested as soon as his EMT helped him to his feet. "And you can ride in the ambulance with her. I'll follow in my car so I can bring you both home after."

"We'll take a taxi back," Camry told him, holding the blanket up to her chest. She looked at Luke's EMT. "He shouldn't be driving, should he?"

"No."

Camry finally found her smile, and she made sure it was damn smug. Fiona might have put the idea in Luke's head that she might welcome his attention by giving him her number, but she'd be damned if she was entertaining some bored tourist on sabbatical.

"I'd offer to drive you home from the hospital," Dave said, walking over to the gurney. He waved toward the police talking to people lined up to get their vouchers. "But I'm afraid I'm going to be tied up here until the wee hours." He stepped closer. "Wipe that smirk off your face, MacKeage. The guy did rescue our little girl, after all," he whispered.

"I don't like pushy men," she whispered back. "And I sure as hell don't want to encourage them by being nice."

Dave snorted. "I can see that's been working well for you."

Chapter Six

Camry woke up to a wet tongue slobbering in her ear, but wasn't alarmed because she recognized Max's doggie breath. She rolled away with a groan, unwilling to open her eyes for fear of increasing the throbbing in her temple.

That is, until she rolled into a body that wasn't canine. She sat up with a start, grabbed her head to keep it from splitting wide open, and fell back against the pillow with an even louder groan.

"What is licking my face?" Luke Pascal rasped from beside her. "I know it's not your tongue, MacKeage, because it's way too friendly."

"That's Ruffles," she muttered. "And she's a

shameless hussy. Is there a reason you're in my bed, Pascal? Not that it matters, because if you're not out of it in two seconds, I'm going to blacken your other eye."

"Give me a minute, would you? My head is killing me, and I'm afraid a rib will pierce my lung if I move right now."

"What are you doing here?"

"I heard you whimpering in the night, so I came in and checked on you. I must have fallen asleep before I could leave."

"That's a flat-out lie, because I never whimper."

"What in hell did they give us at the hospital?"

"Obviously some very powerful pain pills. Um . . . you don't happen to have any spare ones in your pocket, do you?"

"Boxers don't have pockets."

"I have some for both of you. Max, get down," Fiona said, walking up to Camry's side of the bed. "You, too, Ruffles. Go on, shoo!"

Camry felt the bed dip and cracked open her one good eye to see Fiona holding a pill and a glass of water. Cam opened her mouth and the girl popped in the pill, then lifted her head to give her a drink. As soon as she was done, Fiona got up and headed around the bed to do the same for Luke.

"The doctor warned me that you'd both be

pretty sore this morning. Max! I told you to go in the living room!"

"Whisper," Cam whispered.

"Sorry."

"Why is Luke here?" Cam asked.

"The nice EMT from the ambulance called his wife, and they both hung out in the waiting room with me. Then they gave us a ride home and helped me get you both settled in for the night. John put Luke in my bed, and his wife, Glenna, helped me put you in yours. I slept on the couch, so I don't know how you two ended up in bed together," she finished, sounding way too delighted.

"No, I mean why is Luke in my *house*?"

"Oh, that. When the doctor gave me instructions for both of you, I figured Luke should come stay with us for a few days." She smiled at Cam's one-eyed glare. "After he so gallantly came to my rescue last night, I thought it was the least we could do."

"*He* doesn't care to be talked about as if *he* isn't here," Luke said. "And thank you," he muttered, only to groan when Tigger jumped up on the bed, jostling them both. "How the hell many dogs do you own, anyway?"

"None," Cam told him. "But I babysit four."

"You babysit dogs? Why?"

"To pay the bills."

Camry heard Fiona sigh. "She's still trying to decide what she wants to be when she grows up."

"Excuse me?" Luke said.

"Right now she's torn between being Suzy Homemaker or president of the United States. I told her she's smart enough to be a rocket scientist if she wanted, but she doesn't think that would be all that exciting."

Apparently Luke was so impressed, he couldn't comment.

Cam felt her arm being patted, and found Fiona standing beside her again. "Don't worry about the dogs. I'll take them for their runs for the next few days. The doctor said you need to stay off that ankle."

She looked over at Luke, then back at Cam. "And Luke's got some badly bruised ribs, and Doctor Griswell said they'll probably hurt worse than if they were broken." She grinned. "But don't worry; he sent you both home with plenty of pain pills."

"Can he at least walk back to his own bed?" Cam asked.

"*He* can, just as soon as Fiona leaves," Luke said. "Because *he* is only wearing boxer shorts."

Fiona swept Tigger into her arms, spun around with a giggle, and left.

Luke still didn't move.

"She's gone."

"I know. How about giving me enough time for the pill to kick in?"

"You get five minutes, Pascal."

"So, you babysit dogs and wait tables for a living?"

"No, I babysit dogs through the week and tend bar on the weekends. I was just waiting tables last night so I could keep an eye on Fiona."

"How long has she been . . . missing?"

"I found her on the beach this past Friday. She told me she'd run away from home four days prior to that."

"And you can't get her to tell you anything about her family?"

"No. And I don't dare push her, because I'm afraid she'll run away from *me*."

"Christ, her parents must be going out of their minds. Did you at least call the police to see if they have a missing child reported?"

"First thing Friday, while she was taking a shower. They said no one fitting Fiona's description had been reported missing. Um . . . thank you for rescuing her last night. Dave's right, a lot of men wouldn't have gotten involved, especially considering there were four of those drunken jerks. Hell, there were plenty of other men sitting right there last night, but I didn't see any of them jump out of their seats."

"I have a half sister about Fiona's age."

"Fiona said you're on sabbatical. From what?"

He was silent for several heartbeats, then softly chuckled. "Would you believe rocket science?"

Camry went perfectly still, not even daring to breathe as she tried to calculate the odds of two physicists getting into a barroom brawl and winding up in the same bed the next morning.

"And you know what?" he continued. "Contrary to what you told Fiona, I happen to believe it's an exciting profession."

"How can crunching numbers until your eyes cross be exciting? Especially if those numbers suddenly stop making a lick of sense?"

"You know something about mathematical physics, do you?"

"I know it must be frustrating as hell."

"And babysitting other people's dogs is exciting?"

"The dogs don't question every damn thing I say in an e-mail, or *kindly* point out my mistakes."

"I didn't know dogs used e-mail," he said, amusement lacing his voice.

Camry gave him a shove. "The pill's obviously working now."

"Ow, my ribs! It definitely *isn't* working yet."

"Sorry."

She felt the bed jostle and cracked open her eye just enough to see that he'd rolled toward her, propping his head on his hand. "So you babysit dogs because they think you're the smartest thing since sliced bread, is that it? You don't care to have an engaging argument with a worthy opponent once in a while?"

Camry pulled the blanket up to her chin and tucked it down between them. "I like a good argument when the person I'm arguing with isn't so full of himself that he insists on coming to America to set me straight in person."

"Hmm, I'm a little lost here. I thought we were talking about arguing in general, but you seem to be talking about something a bit more specific. Mind elaborating?"

"No. Go away, Pascal."

He eased back onto his pillow and sighed. "I'm hungry. I never did get supper last night."

"There's some mayonnaise in the fridge. You're welcome to it."

"That's it? You don't cook?"

"Why bother, when I can just go to the Go Back Grill?"

"Maybe you should lean more toward being president when you grow up, instead of Suzy

Homemaker." He sighed again. "I don't suppose anyone delivers in this half-deserted town. Maybe Dave or one of his waitresses could bring something over to us."

"Dave brought Cam's SUV home last night," Fiona said, walking back into the bedroom carrying a tray of food and setting it down between them.

Cam slowly sat up, the smell making her mouth water. "He brought food, too?"

"No, I drove to the grocery store this morning and was able to get back before the mutts arrived," Fiona told her, placing the pillow behind her against the headboard.

"You have a driver's license?"

"Almost," Fiona said, going around to set Luke's pillow in place. "And since those pills will knock both of you out soon, I'll wait until then to run to Luke's hotel and get his stuff. Is your room key in your pants, Luke? What's your room number?"

"You can't drive with *almost* a license," Cam told her. "You're supposed to have an adult with you."

"Don't worry that I'll crash your truck, Cam. I've been driving on tote roads since I was ten," the girl said. "I'll take Suki with me and put your sunglasses on her. She's big enough to look like an adult."

"Tote roads?" Camry said, perking up. "That means you live in western Maine."

"They have tote roads in Aroostook and Washington Counties, too." Fiona caught Tigger in midleap when the dachshund tried to jump on the bed, then headed back out of the room with the dog. She stopped at the door. "I'm going to leave Max and Ruffles here, and I'll take Suki and Tigger with me. Luke, your room number?"

"He's going back to his hotel this morning," Camry told her.

"It's room seven," he said, picking up a piece of toast. "And I haven't unpacked, so you'll find my suitcase on the bed."

"You are *not* moving in here with us."

"You heard what the doctor told Fiona. I'm going to be in a lot of pain for the next few days, and it's not safe to take powerful drugs if there's no one around to make sure I don't maim myself. I need supervision, and since you do, too, we might as well be supervised together."

"That makes perfect sense to me," Fiona said from the doorway. "And I certainly don't mind taking care of the both of you. In fact, it will let me know if I want to be a nurse when I grow up." The young girl, who appeared to be enjoying herself way too much, arched her brows at Camry. "Unlike *someone* around here, I want it all: a career *and* a husband *and* children before my biological clock starts ticking down."

Camry grabbed an orange off the tray to fling at her. "You little brat!"

Luke snatched it out of her hand before she could throw it. "Not the food!"

Camry pointed at Fiona. "You just wait until your daddy gets hold of you, young lady. I intend to be standing right beside him, helping him lecture you. And as soon as I can walk, I'm going through all your belongings to find out his name."

"Too late. I burned everything with my name on it in the fireplace this morning."

Camry gasped, sincerely hurt. "You don't trust me?"

Fiona stepped closer. "Of course I do, Camry. It's Luke I don't trust," she said, rolling her eyes. "I mean, really, he *is* a man."

Luke started to hurl the orange at her, but Camry snatched it out of his hand and began peeling it. Fiona spun away with a laugh, shooed the three other dogs out ahead of her, and closed the bedroom door.

"She's been living with you only a few days, and you've already corrupted her opinion of men," Luke accused, just before taking a bite of his toast.

"I'm pretty sure Fiona had you men figured out long before I found her. She told me she left home because her father wouldn't stop lecturing her."

"Because he loves her."

She stopped ripping into the orange and looked at him. "Why can't men love their wives and daughters without lecturing them to death?"

"How in hell should I know? I've never had a wife or a daughter."

"How about a girlfriend? You got one of those?"

"Not at the moment," he said, staring down at his toast. "I don't seem to have any problem *getting* a girlfriend, I just can't seem to keep one."

"Because you lecture them to death."

"No, that's not it." He picked up the plate of eggs and started eating, talking between bites. "They never stick around long enough for me to reach the lecture stage." He looked over at her. "Assuming there even is one," he said, returning to wolfing down his food.

Camry found herself quite intrigued. She could see why Luke Pascal didn't have trouble getting girlfriends, since Fiona had been dead-on about his being dreamy. He had the body of an athlete—which really didn't go with the physicist thing—and his eyes were a beautiful deep blue. As for his hair, well, she had to admit she did like it long; it gave him a rugged, rebellious look, which also didn't match his profession.

His chest wasn't anything to scoff at, either. His shoulders were broad and his well-defined pecs, liberally sprinkled with soft-looking hair, certainly rang *her* bell.

"So why can't you keep a girlfriend?" she asked, wondering if maybe he bombed in the bedroom. He was a nerd, after all, even if he did have a good deal of brawn.

"According to the women who were still speaking to me when they packed up their toothbrushes, I'm boring. Apparently you ladies need a guy's undivided attention," he said, sounding more confounded than resigned.

Camry almost burst out laughing, but caught herself when she realized he was serious. "So you spent all your time working instead of with your girlfriends?"

"If they wanted to be with me, why didn't they come hang out at my lab?"

Okay, the guy truly was clueless. "Maybe you should try dating other physicists. You know, another scientist who would understand being ignored?"

"Have you *met* many women scientists?" He actually shivered. "They scare the hell out of me."

"They do? How?"

"I can name you three right off the top of my head who pull their hair back so tight, they look like they have botched face-lifts." He shivered again. "And two women come to mind who could probably knock me on my ass in three seconds flat." He snorted. "And a lot of female scientists have the personality of lab rats."

Camry didn't know why, but she found that hilariously funny. "And most of the *male* scientists I've met," she said through her laughter, "couldn't dance their way out of a wet paper bag!"

"Hey, *I* can dance."

"And I've met fish with more personality than most of them have."

Luke started laughing, too. "Okay, you've got me there. So have I."

Camry threw back the covers and started to swing her legs off the bed.

"Hey, where are you going?" he asked, grabbing her arm. "You can't walk."

"I have to use the bathroom."

He grinned. "Me, too. Okay, here's what we'll do. You wait right there, and I'll walk around and help you since I don't have a bum ankle."

"Okay, but I get the bathroom first."

Luke set his plate on the tray between them, then walked around to her side.

Camry nearly fell over, tilting her head to look at him. "You're a lot bigger when you're half naked." Her eyes stopped halfway up, and she reached out and touched his ribs. "Wow, that's one hell of a bruise." Her gaze finally made it to his battered face. "Are you sure you're a physicist? You certainly held your own last night."

"I've been working out," he said, puffing up his chest, only to let it sink with a groan as he cradled his ribs. "Okay. Give me your hand, and don't put any weight on your nakle."

Camry giggled. "I think your pill's working."

"Nope. I can still feel my ribs."

She pulled herself out of bed—thankful that Fiona had put her in flannel pajamas—then clutched his arm as she balanced on her good leg. "My pill isn't working, either. Both my head and nankle hurt. Don't let me fall."

"I won't. You know why, MacKeage?" he asked, leading her to the bathroom.

"Why?"

"Because you're downright pretty when you smile."

She smiled up at him. "You're not so bad yourself, for a physy-ist."

They reached the bathroom, and Camry transferred her weight from his arm to the sink. "Okay. Go away."

"You won't take forever, will you? I really have to go, too," he said.

She waved toward the bedroom. "Pee out the window or something. I don't have any neighbors."

He walked out and Cam closed the door, locked it, and hobbled over to the toilet.

"You know what I think?" Luke called through the bathroom door.

"Gee, I don't have a clue. What?"

"You know that guy you were having the e-mail argument with? I think you should meet him in person."

"So I can punch him in the nose?"

He didn't answer right away. "Did you really think he was full of himself?"

"He was a know-it-all, holier-than-thou, arrogant son of a bitch."

Luke said nothing to that.

"And if I ever do meet him in person, I will cram his laptop down his throat." She snorted. "He's probably five feet three and four hundred pounds, bald as an eagle, and wears Coke bottles for glasses."

"He really pissed you off, didn't he?" Luke said softly.

Done taking care of business, Camry hobbled to the sink, looked in the mirror, and screamed.

The doorknob rattled. "What's wrong? Did you fall?"

"No, I just looked in the mirror," she said with a slightly hysterical laugh, carefully touching her swollen eye.

It sounded like Luke thunked his head against the door. "Dammit, you just scared the hell out of me!"

"I just scared the hell out of myself." She washed and dried her hands, quickly ran her fingers through her rumpled hair, and unlocked the door.

Luke stumbled into the room when she opened it.

"Your turn," she said.

"I just need to wash my hands and throw some water on my face."

"Why?"

He grinned crookedly. "I peed out the window."

"I was *kidding.*"

"You were taking too long," he said, stepping around her to use the sink.

She'd give him credit, he didn't scream when he looked in the mirror, but he did gasp.

"Aren't we a pair?" she asked, smiling at him in the mirror. "At least we've got two good eyes between us, and you can walk and I can . . . I can . . ."

She hung her head. "I can never go into another bar. Every time I get into trouble, it's in a bar."

He lifted her chin with his finger. "You can go with me. I won't let you get into trouble."

"Said the spider to the fly."

"Smile again."

"No. It hurts my face."

"Because of your shiner, or just when you're around men in general?"

"Hey, I am a *happy* person, dammit."

"Wow, that pill sure wore off fast. Should I ask Fiona to give you another one?"

Camry reached up and grabbed his ears, pulled down his head, then kissed him full on the mouth. "There!" she snapped. "Is *that* happy enough for you?"

He pulled her into his arms, cradled her head against his shoulder, and kissed her back—a bit more forcefully, quite a bit longer, and definitely . . .

Okay, he didn't keep losing girlfriends because he bombed in the bedroom. This guy could *kiss*.

But then, so could she. As a matter of fact, she had perfected kissing.

Camry went weak in the knees—especially the one holding her weight—and sagged against him when his tongue started doing delicious things to hers. She nearly burst into tears when he suddenly pulled away.

"Christ, you're scary," he rasped, his blue eyes locked on hers.

Her head spun in confusion. "Scary?" she repeated, running her fingertip over his jaw. "How's that?"

He tilted her head back again and started kissing her cheek, then trailed soft, shivering kisses down her neck.

Camry trembled with blossoming passion. Yup, he *definitely* rang her bell.

No, wait, there was a *real* bell ringing somewhere.

She pulled away. "Oh my God, what time is it? That's my mother!"

"You have a mother?" Luke muttered, trying to kiss her again, the evidence of his own blossoming passion poking her belly. "She'll call back."

Camry untangled herself from his embrace and hobbled toward her bed. "But if I don't answer, she'll call my lab." She suddenly changed directions when she realized her cell phone wasn't on her nightstand. "Come on, where in hell are you?" She looked around the room, honed in on the bureau, and snatched up her purse.

"Hi, Mom," she said as soon as she flipped open her cell phone. "Gee, is it Monday already? I've been so involved in my work, I don't even know what day it is."

She jumped when Luke took hold of her arm, then let him help her to the bed so she could sit down. "Really?" she said into the phone as she waved him away. "Three feet? It's early for that much snow, isn't it? But it's good for the ski business."

She frowned at Luke when, instead of leaving, he walked around and sat down on his side of the bed and started eating her orange.

"Um, Mom? Could you hold on a minute? Someone just walked in. Stay on the line—this will only take a minute."

She found the Mute button and held it down with her thumb, then snatched her orange from him. "Can't you see I'm having a personal conversation here? Go back to your own bed."

"But it's small. And the damn thing's too short for me." He picked up the toast on her plate of scrambled eggs and dismissed her with a wave. "Don't let me stop you. I'm just going to finish my breakfast and have a nap."

"You are not sleeping in my bed."

"It'll be easier for Fiona if we're both in the same room."

She arched a brow. "So you wouldn't mind if *your* baby sister took care of two virtual strangers sharing the same bed?"

He scowled at her, then stuffed his mouth full of toast.

Camry released the Mute button and held the phone back to her ear. "Can I call you back later, Mom? There's something going on here that needs my undivided attention. What?" She sighed. "Yeah, I'm afraid I still can't make it home for the solstice. I know, but better than anyone, you should understand how this work goes. I really don't dare lose my focus for that long. And I can't work at home during the holidays because of all the chaos. Okay, I'll talk to you later. Yes, I love you, too. Bye, Mom. Tell Daddy I love him," she said in a rush, just before hitting the End button.

"You're not going home for Christmas?" Luke asked, taking another bite of toast.

Camry stuffed what was left of her orange in her mouth.

"Wait, you said if you didn't answer, your mom would call your *lab*. You have a lab?" He made a production of looking at all the doors in the room, then pointed at the closet door. "Is it in there? What kind of lab is it?" He gasped dramatically. "Not a *meth* lab!" He shook his head. "And you're worried about what impression our being in the same bed will have on Fiona."

"Will you get real? Better yet, get out of here."

"What kind of lab were you talking about, MacKeage?"

She settled back against the headboard with a sigh, and pushed around her eggs with a fork. "I used to be a rocket propulsion physicist."

"You're a rocket scientist? For real? Wait, you said used to be. As in you're *not* a physicist anymore?" He grinned. "What happened, did you suddenly forget how to count past ten without undressing your feet?"

She glared over at him. "No, I got stuck."

"Stuck?" He snorted. "Real scientists don't get stuck, MacKeage. We hit brick walls sometimes, but we either find a way around them or start digging through them. Wait," he said, snapping his fingers. "Did your brick wall have anything to do with that guy you were having the e-mail argument with?"

"The arrogant bastard sent me an equation that completely contradicted three years of my work," she growled, throwing the fork across the room, where it hit the wall and clattered to the floor. "And then he had the audacity to suggest we should work on the problem *together*."

"So, are you angry because a fellow scientist wants to work with you, or because the equation he sent you was correct?"

"His name is Lucian Renoir. God, even his name sounds arrogant. But I'm the one who's going to give the world a viable ion propulsion system," she said, slapping her chest, "whereas he just wants to come here and steal my work."

"Um, there's a bit of a flaw in your theory, MacKeage. He can't steal what doesn't exist. You walked away, remember?" He suddenly smiled at her. "But if you think this Renoir fellow is five feet three and weighs four hundred pounds, maybe you're expecting him to croak any minute, and then you'll start working again?"

Since she'd thrown the fork, Camry used her fingers to eat some of the scrambled eggs. "I can't start up again if I can't figure out how to get un-stuck." She glanced at him, then looked back at the tray. "He . . . the equation he sent me was correct. I had to retrace nearly two years of work before I found where I'd shot off on a tangent." She looked over at him. "But even though I found the problem, I still can't figure out how to fix it."

"Maybe Renoir could help you."

"But if he can make it work, then I should be able to, too." She actually smiled. "But I doubt he can do it on his own, because he's really not all that bright."

"He's not?"

"He can't even figure out that my mother is Dr. Grace Sutter."

"*The* Dr. Sutter, who used to work for StarShip Spaceline? Hell, I've read all her papers. She's the one who turned me on to space science when I was twelve."

Cam snorted. "She turned me on to it in her womb."

"So why aren't you collaborating with her?"

She looked back down at the tray and frowned. "I've tried, but she refuses. She just suddenly walked away from ion propulsion when I was a kid, and started locking herself in her lab to work on something else." She snorted. "Probably cookie recipes. Having seven daughters seems to have taken the edge off her passion for science." She looked over at him. "You men don't have to worry about pregnancies messing you up with nurturing hormones, so you never lose your edge."

His navy blue eyes studied her for several heartbeats. "Is that what you think happened to your mother?"

"What else could it be? She was really close to perfecting ion propulsion when she met my father and started having babies, and, thirty-five years later, we *still* don't have a viable system."

"But the paper I read was written . . ." He looked away in thought. "I was around twelve then, and I'm thirty-three now." He looked back at her. "Your mother was still publishing just twenty years ago. And I believe she's published as recently as six years ago, though not on ion propulsion. She's still in the game, Camry. At least *she* didn't just suddenly walk away to start bartending and babysitting dogs."

Cam said nothing as she looked down at the tray again.

"What really made you walk away, MacKeage?" His eyes suddenly widened. "Does it have something to do with what Fiona said just a minute ago? Maybe you're not standing in front of a brick wall, but are smack in the middle of a midlife crisis." He pointed at the bedroom door. "When you were Fiona's age, didn't you want it all, too: a career *and* a husband *and* children? But where you had one out of the three, now you have none." He suddenly smiled. "Or are you really on sabbatical, working on goals two and three?"

"I don't ever intend to get married and have children."

"Not ever? That's a hell of a long time."

"I don't see you rushing out to get yourself a wife and children."

He let out a huge yawn and suddenly scooted down in the bed. "I would probably be married right now if I could keep a girlfriend long enough to propose to her. I just can't seem to find one who gets turned on by what I do."

Camry glared at him, even though his eyes were closed. But then she also let out a yawn.

She started to shove the tray toward him to make room for herself, only to suddenly remember his bruised ribs. She set the tray on the floor beside the bed, slid down under the blankets, and turned her back to him.

Maybe instead of ion propulsion, she should work on the science of *men* having babies, so Mother Nature could screw with their hormones for a change.

Chapter Seven

Luke sat sprawled on the couch four days later, watching the infomercial explaining how mineral-based makeup would make his skin feel like he wasn't wearing anything, so bored out of his skull he was damn close to tears.

How in hell did Camry do this five days a week, week after week?

Granted, the dogs were entertaining—for all of ten minutes—but how did she just hang around this house all day, doing virtually nothing? How does anyone with even half a brain not justify the air they breathe by at least trying to be productive?

When she'd mentioned her e-mail argument

that first morning, Luke had felt guilty that he
might have been responsible for Camry's walking
away from her work. But as he'd gotten to know
her over the last four days, he'd come to realize
that her little midlife crisis had more to do with her
mother—and her concept of family in general—
than it had to do with him or her work.

He now believed that Camry was afraid of
being just like her mother instead of wanting to
emulate her, afraid that falling in love with a man
and having babies would addle her brain, and
afraid of losing her passion for the sciences—
which she readily admitted she'd acquired in the
womb—just like she believed her mother had.

And Luke was pretty sure that being afraid of
anything was as mind-boggling to Camry Mac-
Keage as doing nothing all day was to him.

That's why he'd spent the last four days trying
to figure out how he might jump-start Camry—
not only back into her work, but also back to her
family. Admitting he was Lucian Renoir certainly
might do the trick, but he wasn't convinced it
wouldn't just as easily push her in the opposite
direction.

Unless he also confessed that he'd destroyed
her mother's satellite. Because if that didn't make
her want to kill him in his sleep, maybe she'd at
least try to kill him in the scientific arena.

Not that it mattered, considering he'd committed professional suicide the moment he'd started eavesdropping on Podly.

Luke drove his hand into the cellophane bag Fiona had given him before she'd gone to help Camry take a shower, and pulled out a fistful of corn chips. Four heads lifted and eight ears perked up. Four drooling tongues appeared, and eight hopeful brown eyes locked on his hand moving toward his mouth.

Luke suddenly lifted his hand over his head, then darted it to the side, then quickly shot it over to his other side—all the while watching the canine eating machines track his movements with the intensity of a guided missile locked on its target.

"You are such uncomplicated beasts," he muttered, tossing the chips to the floor.

While they were occupied chomping down the junk food and inhaling stray crumbs up their noses, Luke quietly reached into the bag again and quickly filled his own mouth as he absently watched the magical transformation as a woman's face went from blotchy red to visibly flawless.

Camry MacKeage certainly didn't need this product; she hadn't been wearing any makeup that first morning he'd awakened beside her, and her skin had looked damned flawless to him—except for the bruise on her left cheek and around her eye, which was only now starting to fade.

She'd felt pretty damn good in his arms, too, when she had recklessly kissed him right there in the bathroom, and he had just as recklessly kissed her back.

When he'd decided to come to America, Luke had known Camry was somewhere around five feet three, but had hoped *her* weight had blossomed to four hundred pounds. And it wouldn't have hurt, either, if she'd sprouted horns soon after the photo had been taken that he'd found of her on the Internet. Considering his track record with women, he'd have preferred that Dr. MacKeage be anything but gorgeous, because he hadn't wanted even a hint of sexual tension to creep into their work.

So much for that pipe dream. Hell, if they both hadn't been so beaten up that first morning, he wouldn't be bored to tears right now because he would have spent the last four days making love to her.

Not that he hadn't tried.

It had become somewhat of a game between them—or maybe *challenge* was a better word— where they flirted right up to the edge of full-blown passion, then withdrew into what Luke could only describe as salacious hell. He was so sexually frustrated, and so damned *in lust* with Camry MacKeage, that the next time she kissed him he wasn't going to care if the dogs watched, he intended to take her right here on the couch.

Hell, he'd nearly nailed her this morning, when he'd awakened to find *her* in *his* bed. Looking him straight in the face with the same piercing green eyes as her father, she'd had the nerve to say she'd heard him whimpering in his sleep but had fallen asleep before she could return to her bed.

Fiona, apparently not the least bit impressionable, had breezed in, popped a pill in each of their mouths, and told them she was running out to buy groceries. Beginning to suspect the romantically inclined teenager was keeping them drugged so they would keep playing musical beds, Luke had started hiding his pill in his cheek, then slipping it behind the headboard the moment the girl turned her back.

If Camry had a mouse problem, they were certainly happy rodents now.

In an attempt to distract himself from his raging lust, Luke had tried focusing on Fiona instead, specifically on finding out her last name so he could locate her parents. But apparently teens today were much sharper than he had been, because when *he* had run away from home, he hadn't made it ten miles before his stepfather had found him. André had dragged Luke home, handed him a crosscut saw and ax, and made him cut, chop, and stack eight cords of firewood by hand while he contemplated the hell he had put his mother through.

Luke hadn't run away from home again until age twenty-four.

He heard the bedroom door open and knew that Camry—likely armored in lilac-scented soap for another one of their salacious battles—was heading over to sit down beside him while Fiona took the dogs out for their morning walk. The winter solstice was only a week away, and Luke figured he had only one or two days left to talk Camry into going home before she claimed he was fully recovered and kicked him out on his sexually frustrated ass.

He sighed, scooting over to make room for her on the couch as he patted his pocket to make sure he'd remembered the condoms. It was time, he'd decided this morning while shaving, to launch a full frontal attack: first on Camry's body—because he really, painfully wanted her—and then on her conscience.

"I'm heading out to walk the mutts," Fiona said as she put on her jacket. "Is there anything either of you need before I go?"

"A beer would be nice," Luke said, not caring if it was only ten in the morning, because he was so damned bored. Dave had brought him a six-pack, but Fiona had hidden it, claiming he couldn't mix beer with the drugs she thought he was still taking.

"If you don't take your afternoon pill, you can have one tonight with supper," she promised, snapping leashes on the four tail-wagging dogs and heading outside.

"You seem to be getting around quite well," Luke said when Camry swiped his bag of corn chips. "How's the ankle feeling?"

"Ready to run a marathon," she said, stuffing her mouth with chips.

"Are you going to waste time eating, or can we go straight to the necking part of this morning's entertainment? They'll only be gone an hour."

She looked over at him, blinking her pretty green eyes, and Luke realized there had been an edge in his voice. He grinned. "Or we can skip the necking and just kick things up a notch. But I suggest we use your bed, because the spare really isn't large enough for the two of us—as you found out this morning, when I gallantly saved you from falling out on your sexy little . . . behind."

She blinked at him again.

Okay, so maybe *direct* wasn't the best approach after all. He threw his arm over the back of the couch behind her, drove his other hand into the bag of chips, and munched away while he waited for her to make the first move.

Assuming she made it in five minutes. He figured he needed at least forty-five minutes in the bedroom, and that gave him only ten minutes' leeway in case Fiona walked fast today.

Camry attacked him in three.

The bag of junk food suddenly went flying and she scrambled onto his lap; before he'd even finishing swallowing, she cupped his face in her delicate hands and kissed him. Quickly recovering from the surprising assault, Luke wrapped his arms around her and let her have her wicked way with him, because . . .

Well, because just as soon as she got herself worked into a really good frenzy, he was hopefully going to use two of the three condoms in his pocket.

And once she was so exhausted she couldn't speak, and hopefully too mellow to care, then he would casually mention who he actually was.

Then he'd tell her what he'd done to Podly.

And then he would very nicely ask her to help him find the little satellite so they could bring it back to her mother, and the three of them could lock themselves in Gù Brath's lab until they had a viable propulsion system to present to the world.

Realizing he was about to pop the zipper on his jeans, and seeing how Camry had his shirt unbuttoned and was doing wickedly delightful things to his nipples with her tongue, Luke cupped her backside, stood up, and headed toward her bedroom.

She didn't even notice the sudden change of venue, she was so busy working herself into a frenzy. And when he laid her on the bed, settled his sexually frustrated body beside her, and started undoing her blouse, she very kindly helped.

Surprised he even had the sense of mind to glance at the clock on the nightstand, Luke gave himself five minutes to get her naked.

Only she had him naked in two. And herself naked in one.

Luke began to wonder who was seducing whom.

"Beautiful," he murmured, his mouth trailing down her throat on its way to her lovely breasts, and his hands . . . hell, he simply touched her everywhere, since every damn square inch of her turned him on.

Though he thought she had already worked herself into quite a frenzy, Luke discovered she was only getting started. Camry turned so suddenly wild and urgently aggressive, she reminded him of the blizzard that had all but immobilized him for two entire days with its intensity.

She didn't waste time exploring any parts of his body that didn't seem immensely interesting. Her hands went straight to his groin, and Luke pretty near bucked them off the bed when she wrapped her fingers around him.

Where in hell had she thrown his pants with the condoms?

Alarmed to see her head dipping in the same direction as her hands, and fearing four days of building frustration would be over in three seconds if he didn't get her under control, Luke took hold of her shoulders and hauled her up beside him.

But then he had to pin her hands over her head and throw his leg over hers to keep *her* from bucking them off the bed.

"Slow down," he rasped, trying to catch his breath.

She was also panting, as if she really had run a marathon, and Luke worried that if just getting naked left them both winded, full-blown sex might actually kill them.

He slid his free hand down her ribs to her pelvis, and found her moist and hot and definitely ready for him.

Where in hell were his pants!

She made a ragged sound of pleasure and arched into his touch. Luke increased the pressure and slid a finger inside her, retreated, and repeated the intoxicating dance. She tightened around him, her body humming with building tension as she strained against his hold on her wrists. Her climax was as sudden and gloriously breathtaking as an exploding nova.

And it didn't slow her down one damn bit.

So caught up in the wave of pleasure he was witnessing, Luke didn't realize he'd slackened his grip. And before he knew it, Camry's hands were back at his groin, doing gloriously breathtaking things to him.

And just as suddenly as she had, he made an utter disgrace of himself.

He flopped back on the bed beside her with a groan and stared up at the ceiling, trying to catch his breath as he wondered what had just happened.

Little Miss Exploding Nova, also panting raggedly, rolled over and snuggled against him with a sigh. She patted his chest. "Thanks. I really needed that."

Chapter Eight

*L*uke pulled the unused condoms out of his pants pocket two mornings later and tossed them in his ditty bag with a derisive snort. He'd just experienced two days of the best sex of his life, and he hadn't even gotten to use one of the damn things. He still couldn't figure out how he could be so sexually sated without technically having sex, or how Camry MacKeage had managed to fool him into believing he *was*.

Dammit, what sort of perverted game was she playing? They'd done it every way but standing on their heads, but they hadn't actually done it!

Luke suddenly reached in the ditty bag, pulled out one of the condoms, and stuffed it back in his pocket. He was on to her now, by God, and he'd be damned if he was going to be used as some convenient boy toy to stave off *her* boredom.

The very next time they got naked together he was calling her bluff, and either she could put out for real, or he was taking the next flight back to France. To hell with her and this whole damn mess. He'd been deluding himself long enough, holding out hope there was anything left of that damn satellite worth salvaging. And being in lust with a woman was one thing, but deliberately being used by her was . . . it was . . .

Dammit, he actually felt violated!

Fired up with righteous indignation and no small amount of wounded pride, Luke stormed out of the bathroom in search of the green-eyed siren.

Only finding the house was empty, he stood in the living room, nonplussed. Fiona must have taken the dogs out for their walk early, and Camry must have gone with her. Dammit to hell! Had she grown bored with him already?

But wait. She couldn't stay out the entire hour; her ankle still wasn't that strong. Luke grabbed his jacket, fully intending to sit on the steps and ambush her when she returned. Only he nearly fell over her when he rushed out the porch door, because Camry was sitting on the top step. She didn't even bother looking up when he bumped into her, but simply continued to stare down at something in her hand.

Immediately sensing something was wrong, Luke silently sat down beside her. It was then he noticed she was holding open a card. And though he couldn't quite read it, the handwriting looked eerily familiar. When Camry still didn't acknowledge he was there, he glanced around for Fiona, even standing up to see the beach, looking in both directions for the girl.

"She's gone," Camry said, her voice lacking any emotion.

Luke sat back down. "She took all the dogs to the grocery store?"

"The dogs don't come on Saturdays."

He glanced at Camry with growing alarm. "Will she be back soon?"

"She's not coming back."

The hair on his neck stood up, his gut tightened painfully, and every muscle in his body tensed. "She ran off?" he whispered. He stood up again. "Come on then, we have to go find her. I don't care how mature she seems, we can't let her wander around alone!"

Camry still didn't move. "She's okay. She's gone . . . home."

Luke took a deep breath in an attempt to control

his pounding heart and sat back down beside her with a disheartened sigh. "All she left us was a card? She couldn't even say good-bye in person?"

Camry reached down between her knees, her hand returning with an envelope, and Luke finally noticed the small box sitting on the step below her, between her feet.

"Fiona left you this," she said, handing him the envelope.

His heart started pounding again when he saw his name—*Lucian Pascal Renoir*—in flourished handwriting that was definitely familiar. He glanced over at Camry, but she continued to stare out at the ocean. He slid his finger under the sealed flap and pulled out a card exactly like the one Grace and Greylen MacKeage had received over a week ago.

He opened it. *Please don't give up on her,* Luke silently read, *because everyone needs a miracle once in a while, and you are hers.* She'd drawn a little smiley face, then continued. *And though you might find it hard to believe right now, she is your miracle. Have a great adventure together, you two. I'll see you again . . . sooner than you think.* She'd drawn another smiley face, before signing, *All my love, Fiona Gregor.*

Luke lifted his gaze to the ocean. *Gregor.* Why did that name sound familiar?

Fiona Gregor.

"Don't you have a brother-in-law named Gregor?" he asked.

"Matt. He's married to my sister Winter," Camry said, still looking out to sea. "Fiona's their daughter. And my niece."

He frowned at her. "You didn't recognize your own niece?"

She dropped her gaze to the card in her hand. "I didn't recognize her because right now she's only five and a half months old."

Luke's heart started trying to pound out of his chest again. He didn't know which alarmed him more: what Camry was saying, or her utter lack of emotion. She had obviously read his name on the envelope she'd handed him, so she knew exactly who he was. Why wasn't she going for his jugular, or at least screaming her head off?

And what in hell did she mean, Fiona was only five months old?

This had to be some sort of bizarre joke.

And how had Fiona found out his full name, anyway?

He snorted. "Apparently our respecting the little brat enough not to go through her belongings wasn't reciprocated. She obviously went through my briefcase when she picked it up for me."

He held the envelope with his name on it in

front of Camry, but when she still didn't respond, he dropped his hand back on his thigh. "I know you probably won't believe me, but I was going to tell you today." He shifted uncomfortably, disguising the action by sliding the card back in its envelope. "In fact, I've spent all week trying to figure out how to tell you. I . . . you should also know that your mother asked me to come here and talk you into going home for Christmas."

She finally looked at him, her eyes filled with horror. "Mom *knows* I'm living in Maine?" she whispered. "D-does Daddy know, too?"

Luke nodded.

She was on her feet and off the steps so fast, it took him a moment to realize she was bolting. The colorfully wrapped box clattered down the steps after her, the card she'd been holding trailing behind it.

Luke jumped to his feet and ran after her. "Camry!" he shouted, tearing onto the beach, amazed she could run so fast on her ankle. "Wait! Let me explain! Dammit, will you stop! You're going to hurt your ankle again!"

It took him an amazingly long time to catch her, and then he had to tackle her to get her to stop, twisting so he took the brunt of their fall. But then he was forced to protect himself from her pummeling fists, his heart nearly stopping when he realized she was sobbing as she lashed out at him.

He finally just hugged her so tightly that her blows became ineffective, and cupped her head to his cheek. "Shhh," he crooned, wrapping his legs around hers to stop her struggles. "It's okay. Everything's going to be okay."

She suddenly went limp. "Let me go."

He chuckled humorlessly. "Not a chance, lady. Just listen to me, will you?" he said in a rush when she started struggling again. "I just spent the last two months searching Springy Mountain for your mother's satellite, which crashed there last summer."

She went still again, only this time she remained guardedly tense.

"But I got caught in a blizzard, and your brother-in-law Jack Stone found me and brought me to your parents," he quickly continued. "I told them who I was. Well, I told them I was Luke Pascal, but I did say I was the man you'd been corresponding with all last winter. Anyway, I wasn't aware they didn't know you no longer worked for NASA, so you can blame that one on me. But it was Fiona who sent them a Christmas card, which led them to believe you were living here in Go Back Cove."

He shrugged, shrugging her with him. "I don't

know why they refused to come get you themselves. But your mother said something about
their needing you to *want* to come home. So she
asked me to come get you."

He sighed, pressing his face into her hair. "I
don't know if any of this is making any sense,
Camry, or even getting through to you. I only
know that your parents love you immensely, and
they're . . . aw hell, they're hurt and confused and
probably scared sick that you've been keeping
your secret from them for so long."

She went completely limp again, and this time
Luke knew she wasn't faking. It might have had
something to do with her silent sobs, or the fact
that instead of pushing him away, she was now
clutching him with wrenching desperation.

He slid his fingers through her hair. "I'm sorry,"
he murmured. "I am so damned sorry for not
telling you up front who I was, and I'm sorry for
letting your parents talk me into coming after you
in the first place. This was none of my business,
really, but since I'm rather invested now, I have to
ask: Why couldn't you tell your mother what was
going on with your work?"

He slackened his hold just enough to lift her
chin, and his heart nearly stopped again at the
pain he saw in her eyes. He brushed a tear off her
cheek and smiled tenderly. "You have my word,

MacKeage: I won't run home to your mama and tattle. That's completely between you and her. But having met Grace, and seeing how much she loves you, I can't figure out why you couldn't go to her with your problem." He widened his smile. "As for your father, that man scares the hell out of me almost as much as you do."

She blinked at him, and Luke took a relieved breath, figuring he'd gotten them past the worst part. He slackened his hold even more, and when she didn't start swinging at him, he released her totally, gently rolled her off him, and sat up. But when she tried to stand, he took hold of her wrist and held her sitting beside him.

"Just a minute. There's a bit more you need to hear."

She didn't try to break his grip, but simply stared out at the ocean.

Luke took a deep breath. "I had been eaves-dropping on your mother's satellite for several months before I started corresponding with you. I was fascinated with what your mother was doing, and have been working on the same problem myself for nearly ten years. I know what I did was unconscionable, but I was getting so frustrated and so damned desperate, I simply didn't care anymore."

He looked over at her. "I swear, it wasn't my

intention to steal your mother's work; I just wanted to find something—anything—that would move my own work along. But last summer something went terribly wrong, and Podly suddenly fell out of orbit and crashed just north of Pine Creek. I've spent the last two months searching for it on Springy Mountain, hoping I could take it to Grace so she could salvage some part of her work."

"You don't find it strange that Podly crashed so close to Pine Creek?" she asked, her voice raspy with lingering sobs.

He frowned. "Well, I admit it's more than a little perplexing." He turned to face her fully, and lifted her hand so he could hold it in both of his. "But what I'm trying to tell you is, I am truly, profoundly sorry for what I did. And I'm asking for another chance. Please, let me prove to you that even though nothing could ever justify what I've done, my intentions have always been honorable."

She pulled free, folded her hands on her lap, and stared out at the ocean again.

"Please don't shut me out, Camry. Let me prove my sincerity. Help me find Podly and bring it back to your mother."

"I can't ever go home again," she whispered. She hugged her knees to her chest, huge tears spilling down her cheeks as she continued staring out at the ocean. "I can't face either of them. I've been lying for what seems like forever. I've been lying to my entire family." She dropped her head to her knees. "They'll never forgive me."

Luke leaned down and brushed away a tear with his thumb. "So you're saying that if one of your sisters had a bit of a midlife crisis, then tried to cover it up and deal with it herself, you wouldn't forgive her?"

"You don't understand. This wouldn't happen to one of my sisters. MacKeage women don't have midlife crises, because we're too damn busy being brilliant, successful, and happy."

Luke snorted, then smiled when she glared at him. "Nobody goes through life avoiding brick walls. I'd bet my last dollar that every one of your sisters has hit at least one, if not several, walls." He took hold of her hand again and held it in his. "You may be standing in front of one right now, but it's not the end of the road. If you can't go around it, then you just have to find a way through it. And your mother," he said, giving her a squeeze, "is desperate to help you. And your father . . . well, I bet he'd give his right arm to help you through this." He leaned forward to look her in the eyes. "And so would I, Camry."

She said nothing, pulling her hand away to hug her knees again as she stared out at the ocean.

Luke turned to watch the waves gently lapping toward them. "I sold my soul trying to unlock the secret of ion propulsion, but over the course of this last week, I've decided that I don't give a flying damn about it anymore." He looked over at her and took a deep breath. "Tell me how to help you fix this," he softly petitioned. "I'll do whatever you want . . . except walk away. I'll go home and face your parents with you, or if you prefer, I'll go get them and bring them here. Or I can take you home to my mother in British Columbia and wait until you're ready to go home to yours."

She remained silent, then suddenly got to her feet. "I need to think."

He also scrambled to his feet. "I don't have a problem with that," he offered, falling in step beside her as they headed toward the house. "As long as you understand that I'm not leaving."

Chapter Nine

Camry walked down the beach at a brisk pace, her head feeling like it was going to explode from the tears she desperately fought to hold back. So much had happened this morning, she wasn't sure she'd ever recover. She'd been hit with so many lies and half-truths about so many things—not the least of which was silently walking beside her.

He was *Lucian Renoir*, the man of her dreams and nightmares of over a year.

In her dreams, she had worked side by side with a fantasy version of the handsome physicist, sharing their scientific passions by day and indulging their sexual passions at night.

But she'd also had a recurring nightmare involving an equally handsome Dr. Renoir, where he was standing at a podium as she sat cowered before him wearing nothing but her underwear. He was lecturing her in front of an assembly of their peers, expounding at length on her inability to solve even the simplest equation. Her mother and father, and all her brilliant, successful sisters sat in the front row, their heads hung in shame.

But all her dreams and nightmares combined were nothing compared to Lucian Renoir in the flesh. He was even more handsome than she'd imagined: definitely taller, a heck of a lot leaner, and more rugged-looking than the man in the grainy photo she'd found on the Internet. It was the long hair and ripped body, she guessed, that had prevented her from being suspicious of having bumped into a fellow physicist in the unlikely town of Go Back Cove.

That's why it felt as though she'd taken a punch in the gut this morning, when she had read the name on the card Fiona had left him. Having grown quite fond of Luke as they'd recuperated together, and finding herself more and more sexually attracted to him with each passing day, she had actually started weaving fantasies of following him home at the end of his sabbatical. She better than anyone could handle being ignored when he got involved at his lab, and she had hoped his passion for his work might actually rub off on her, and maybe even nudge her back into the game.

But he wasn't good old Luke Pascal, was he?

He was *Lucian Renoir*. Which brought her right back to her nightmare of sitting cowering on a stage instead of realizing her dream of spending her days in his lab and her nights in his bed.

They reached the porch steps, and Luke picked up the gaily wrapped box that Fiona had left with the cards on the kitchen table, before the girl had vanished as mysteriously as she had appeared only a week ago.

He held the gift out to her, but Camry shoved her hands in her pockets. "It's addressed to both of us," she said. "You open it."

He tucked it under his arm, gathered up the cards that had blown into the tall grass, then walked up the stairs and held open the door. Camry preceded him inside and went directly to her bedroom, closed and locked the door, then threw herself down on the bed and burst into tears.

Luke stood leaning against the kitchen counter, sipping his third beer from the six-pack he'd found in the fridge, and stared at the box he'd placed on the table along with Fiona's two cards.

He just didn't feel right opening the gift without Camry.

He hadn't felt right about reading the note Fiona had left her, either, but since he was already flying down the slippery slope of deceit, he'd read it anyway. He'd actually chuckled, despite feeling like hell, when he discovered the romantic teenager had left Camry a note almost identical to his.

Just as short and idealistic, the young girl's note had asked Camry not to give up on *him,* and she'd echoed that they were each other's miracle. The only deviation had been that Fiona had finished Camry's note by saying that she'd see her favorite *auntie* next week, on the winter solstice.

Luke twisted off the cap on another beer and took a long swig. Christ, the house felt empty without the brat and the mutts. The gut-wrenching sobs coming from the bedroom—which hadn't stopped until he'd heard the shower turn on twenty minutes ago—were the only reminder he wasn't alone.

He honest to God didn't know what to do. His heart ached to see Camry happy, but he couldn't figure out how to make that happen. And he didn't have a clue what he could say to help her find the courage to face her parents. Hell, he was about as much help as were the cryptic notes that Fiona had left them.

A miracle? What in hell did the girl mean, they were each other's miracle? They'd screwed up their own lives so badly, he questioned if they were even competent to babysit the dogs.

Luke straightened when he heard the bedroom door open. He quickly shoved his empty beer bottles back in the holder and put everything back in the fridge except the one he was drinking. But then he grabbed one of the full bottles and set it on the table, and had just made it back to lean against the counter when Camry walked into the kitchen.

She sat down, folded her hands on the table, took a deep breath, and looked at him. "Okay, I'm ready. You can begin," she said, her voice husky. She suddenly held up her hand when he tried to speak. "Only I wish you'd keep it under an hour, because I still have some thinking to do."

"Um . . . begin what?"

"The lecture you've been dying to give me ever since you arrived in Go Back Cove," she said, her tone implying he was a bit dense for making her state the obvious.

"I've been dying to give you a lecture?" he repeated, *feeling* dense. "About what?" He suddenly stiffened. "You want me to lecture you about the mistake in your equation? Camry, I told you, I don't give a flying damn about that anymore."

She gaped at him.

He sighed. "Okay, look. If you want to talk about it we can, but some other time. Right now I'd rather hear from you." He took a swig of liquid courage, then looked back at her. "I really need to know how things stand between us, because I really need for you not to shut me out."

She snapped her mouth closed, opened it several times, as if she were searching for words, then finally whispered, "Are you for real?"

Luke shifted uneasily, then suddenly flinched when she shot out of her chair and rushed up to him. He sucked in his breath when she just as suddenly shoved on his belly at the same time as she pulled out his belt and looked down his pants!

He sidestepped away in alarm. "What *are* you doing?"

"I'm looking to see if you still have your balls."

"My what!" he yelped, stepping even farther away.

She walked back to her chair, sat down, and folded her hands on the table again. "Don't worry, they're still there. So let's get on with it, okay? I told you, I still have some thinking to do."

"Get on with *what*?" he growled, tugging one pants leg.

"Your lecture."

Luke sighed, long and loud and heartfelt. "Will

you please tell me what I'm supposed to be lecturing you on?"

"On what a selfish, inconsiderate daughter I am. While you're expounding on what a no-good rotten liar I am, you might as well get in a few licks on my cowardice."

The lightbulb finally clicked on, and Luke went utterly still, then collapsed into the chair opposite her. "Camry," he said softly. "There is nothing I can or would say to you that you can't or haven't already said to yourself."

She was back to gaping at him.

He shook his head. "You've obviously been beating yourself up over this for an entire year; I'm not about to beat up on you, too." He covered her hands with one of his. "But I can be a damn good team player. You do as much thinking as you need to, but while you're at it, try to think of how I can help you. Whatever course of action you decide on, I'm with you one hundred percent."

"Why?"

He reared back, not having seen that particular question coming.

"Why don't you just walk away?" she elaborated. "Because you said it yourself, this really is none of your business."

"Well, it isn't," he agreed, choosing his words

carefully. "Or it wasn't until . . . sometime around Tuesday, I figure."

"What happened on Tuesday?"

"I fell head over heels in lust with you."

It was her turn to rear back, and, yup, she was gaping at him again.

Luke reached in his pants pocket, pulled out the condom, and set it on the table. "Do you know what this is?"

"It's a condom."

"And do you know what it's used for?"

"Preventing unwanted pregnancies and venereal diseases."

He nodded. "Not bad for a used-to-be scientist. Tell me, have you ever actually seen one out of its packet?" he asked, ripping open the foil.

She leaned back in her chair even farther.

"I only ask because while you were in the bedroom this past hour *thinking,* I was doing a bit of thinking myself. And you know what I was thinking about?" He slid the condom out of its package, then lifted a brow, waiting for her answer.

"N-no," she whispered, her gaze dropping to the condom again.

Luke rolled it open, then left it sitting on the table between them as he picked up the unopened bottle of beer, twisted off the cap, and leaned back in his chair. "I was thinking about how you've perfected the art of satisfying a man in bed so well, he doesn't even realize he's not having intercourse."

She paled to the roots of her beautiful red hair.

He leaned forward to rest his arms on the table. "I think you should know," he continued softly, "that this morning when I realized what had actually been going on the last two days, I wanted to wring your pretty little neck. But sometime in the last hour," he said, motioning toward the bedroom, "everything suddenly made sense."

He leaned even closer, looking her directly in the eyes. "You're a virgin," he said, stating a fact, not asking a question. "You've been so afraid that having a child will steal your passion for your work, you've never been able to go all the way."

"I really don't think that's any of your business."

"You are such a passionate woman, Camry, in and out of bed. Everything you do is full speed ahead, no holds barred, one hundred and ten percent." He leaned back in his chair again. "So to answer your question as to why I don't simply walk away, it's because I can't. For the first time in my adult life, I'm letting my lower brain make my decisions. I'm in lust with you, Camry, and I'm asking you to do what Fiona also asked, and that's for you not to give up on me. Let's solve our problems together."

"I-I don't do commitment well," she whispered, her gaze back on the condom.

"Sure you do," he contradicted, which certainly brought her eyes up to his. "You commit yourself completely, just not long-term. You hit hard and fast, and then you take off before a guy realizes what's happening . . . or rather, what *isn't* happening."

That got the paleness out of her cheeks. She set her hands on the table and stood up, presumably the better to glare down at him. "If you think I'm going to let you blackmail me into having sex, think again, buster."

"Blackmail you!" he said on a strangled laugh. "With what? Hell, *I'm* the one who should worry about being blackmailed. You and your mother have enough dirt on me not only to ruin my career, but to get me thrown in jail for destroying a multimillion-dollar satellite."

She collapsed back in her chair. "My mother knows you were eavesdropping on Podly?"

"From the beginning, apparently," he admitted. "And she also knows that I caused it to crash. Hell, *she's* the blackmailer. She guilted me into coming after you."

Camry buried her face in her hands and

thunked her head down on the table. "What are we going to do?" she muttered. "How am I ever going to face her again?"

Luke nearly jumped up with a shout, he was so happy to hear her speaking in terms of *we*. He did stand up, though, and went to the fridge, pulled out the last bottle of beer, and waited until she'd finally sat up before he handed it to her.

"I have no idea what we're going to do," he said, sitting down again. He slid the gaily wrapped box toward her. "But maybe we should start by opening Fiona's gift. It's possible the meddling little brat left us another cryptic clue. I mean, seeing as how she's so *magical* that she can be five months old and sixteen at the same time."

Camry spit her mouthful of beer all over the gift, the table, and Luke. "Oh God, don't tell me *you* believe in the magic!" she cried, her horrified gaze locked on his.

Luke wiped his cheek with the back of his hand. "What in hell are you talking about? I was kidding, Camry. Fiona—if that's even her real name—obviously found out you had a niece named Fiona Gregor, and decided to mess with your head. She's a *teenager*; it's her job to drive adults crazy. Believe in the magic," he muttered. "What is it with you MacKeages, anyway? I don't believe in magic, serendipitous coincidences, mother's intuition, or miracles. I'm a scientist, and I only believe in what I can back up with cold, hard facts."

Camry absently toyed with the ribbon on the gift as she watched him out the corner of her eye. "So you don't believe it's astronomically impossible that my mother's satellite crashed near her home, or that you arrived at Gù Brath at about the same time Fiona was mailing her card to my parents? And it doesn't seem like a strange coincidence to you that you ran into me within minutes of arriving in Go Back Cove? Or that we ended up in bed together your very first night here, or—"

He held his hand up to stop her. "The odds of all those things happening are huge, I'll admit, but not impossible."

"Okay. Then how about calculating the odds of Podly's crashing into Springy Mountain at the exact time of the summer solstice? Which also happens to be the exact moment—right down to the second, I feel compelled to point out—that Fiona Gregor was born."

He frowned. "That's pushing things a bit much, I think."

She slipped the ribbon off the box, carefully unwrapped the gift, then lifted the cardboard lid just enough to look inside. At first she frowned, then her eyes suddenly widened. She looked up at Luke, spun the box around, and pushed it across the table. "Okay, then explain *that* to me using cold, hard facts."

Luke lifted the flap on the box and also frowned, not quite sure what he was looking at. But then his eyes widened just as Camry's had. He reached in and, as carefully as if he were handling the Holy Grail, he lifted out the slightly charred, fist-sized instrument . . . that actually had the words STARSHIP SPACELINE etched in tiny letters on its side.

"Come on," Camry said smugly, "explain what that piece of Podly is doing in my kitchen, or how a five-month-old *teenager* got her hands on it in the first place, when it should be buried under three feet of snow somewhere on Springy Mountain."

His hands trembling because he was afraid to drop it, Luke carefully set what appeared to be the satellite's transmitter down on the table. "Please tell me I'm dreaming."

"I'm sorry, Luke, I wish I could," she said just as softly. She reached over and picked up the transmitter, which caused him to flinch. She chuckled. "It's already survived a rather long fall," she drawled. "I think it can survive my handling."

She turned it over to study it, and the tiny instrument suddenly chirped.

Camry threw it down as they both jumped in surprise.

The transmitter rolled off the table, and Luke made a lunge for it at the same time she did. But they fell into each other trying to catch it, and the precious instrument clattered to the floor. It rolled across the linoleum, smacked up against the stove, and softly chirped.

Sprawled on their bellies, they both stared at it, utterly speechless.

The damn thing chirped again.

"It's still functioning?" Luke whispered. He looked at her. "Do you suppose there's . . . could more of the satellite have survived, do you think?"

She didn't respond right away, apparently unable to tear her gaze from the transmitter. She finally looked at him, her eyes shining intensely— quite like they did when she was about to rip off his clothes. "I think we're going to have to go to Springy Mountain to answer that question."

"Excuse me?" he whispered, not daring to hope—but hoping anyway.

She straightened to her knees, grabbed their bottles of beer off the table, and handed one to Luke once he sat up to lean against the cupboards. She settled down on the floor beside him and took a long chug of her beer—swallowing this time—then suddenly grinned. "The way I see it, we have three choices. We can break into my family's ski-resort maintenance garage and steal one of the snowcats; we can steal some horses from my cousin Robbie; or we can snowshoe the forty miles to Springy Mountain. Your choice, Dr. Renoir."

She was going home!

And she was taking him with her!

"I have a fourth choice," he carefully offered, not wanting to dampen her spirit—or get himself thrown off her team. "You can go home and tell your parents how much you love them, then *ask* them if we could *borrow* a snowcat. I'm sure they'll be so happy to see you, they will gladly lend us one."

She glared at him.

"What?" he asked, his hopes waning.

"I thought you said you'd do anything to help me."

"I will. I *am*." He ran his hand through his hair, wondering if his lower brain wasn't going to be the death of him. "It's just that I'm pretty sure you and I have both deceived your parents quite enough already. Stealing from them is more or less adding insult to injury, don't you think?"

"Okay then, we'll steal from Robbie," she said, rolling onto her hands and knees and crawling toward the transmitter. "Riding horses into Springy will be colder, but it beats the hell out of snowshoeing."

He grabbed her arm to stop her, then urged her to turn to face him. "Camry, you're going to have to deal with your parents eventually."

"I will, just as soon as we find Podly."

He tightened his grip. "You think you can't go home unless you're bearing gifts?" He shook his head, his eyes never leaving hers. "Take it from a world-class ass of a son and stepson—parents don't want anything from their children but love. And the lesson it took me six stubborn years to learn is that loving them means trusting them."

She blinked at him, then suddenly threw herself at his chest, knocking him back against the cupboards. Luke quickly set down his beer to wrap his arms around her just as she buried her face in his shirt.

He cupped her head to his chest. "It'll be okay, I promise."

"They're never going to forgive me."

"Of course they will. They already have." He lifted her chin. "They're just waiting for you to forgive yourself."

"But you don't understand," she whispered, burying her face again.

"Then explain it to me," he petitioned, holding her tightly against him.

She quietly sighed, saying nothing.

Luke contented himself with just holding her as he stared at the tiny transmitter sitting next to the stove . . . and resigned himself to the fact that he was about to add stealing a snowcat to his growing list of crimes.

Chapter Ten

It had taken Luke less than twenty minutes to throw his belongings in his suitcase, so he'd spent the rest of the afternoon studying Podly's transmitter—which for some reason had stopped chirping. Camry had stayed in her bedroom, supposedly packing, but Luke suspected she'd taken a nap. It was early evening, and they were sitting across the table from each other, eating the only thing he knew how to cook: scrambled eggs and toast.

Or rather, Camry was eating. He was getting one hell of a lesson on letting his lower brain call the shots. "What do you mean, I have to go stay at the hotel?" he repeated. "I thought we were leaving for Pine Creek in the morning?"

"I've decided not to leave until Wednesday." She shoved her fork into her eggs. "Or maybe Tuesday evening, so we'll arrive in Pine Creek around midnight. It'll be easier to steal the snow-cat then."

Dammit, she was ditching him! "Then let's leave tonight," he offered, careful to keep his frustration from showing. "The sooner we get going, the sooner we'll find the rest of Podly. I had the Weather Channel on all afternoon, and they're talking about another snowstorm heading north by Thursday or Friday. With any luck, we can be on and off the mountain before it hits."

She shot him a confounded look. "You said you spent *two months* searching for Podly. You expect that because I'll be with you this time, we're going to drive directly up to the satellite, load it in the snowcat, and be off the mountain in a matter of days? It will probably take us weeks to find where it crashed."

"Then all the more reason to leave now."

"I can't," she muttered, poking her eggs a bit more forcefully. "I have a couple of commitments here I have to deal with first."

"What commitments?"

"I babysit four dogs, remember? I can't just take off all of a sudden and leave my clients without day care."

"They're dogs, Camry, not kids. They can stay home while their masters work, like normal dogs do."

"But I promised Tigger's and Max's owners that I would keep them over the holidays. The Hemples are leaving for England tomorrow, and I'm supposed to have Tigger for an entire month. And Max's mother is leaving on Tuesday for Wisconsin, and she won't be back until after New Year's."

"Call and tell them you have a family emergency or something."

"You want me to *lie* to them?"

Luke very kindly refrained from pointing out that she'd been lying to her parents for almost a year. "Then let's get on the phone and find alternative accommodations for their pets. Surely there are kennels around here."

"Tigger can't stay in a kennel! She'd be scarred for life. And so would Max. Why do you think these people have me babysit them? They're not dogs, they're *family*."

Luke sighed, not wanting to ask his next question, but seeing how his lower brain was in charge, he asked it anyway. "So what's your plan, then?"

She looked back down at her eggs. "We're going to have to take Tigger and Max with us," she said, so quietly that Luke had to lean forward to hear her.

He reared back. "You expect to take two dogs to Springy Mountain in the middle of the winter? Camry, the snow's deeper than Tigger is tall. And the snowcat's going to be crowded enough with the two of us and our gear. Where are you planning to put Max? He's the size of person."

"We can carry most of our gear on the roof, and we'll steal one of the resort's larger groomers. That way we can even sleep in it if we have to."

Luke dropped his head in his hands to stare down at his plate. Had she changed her mind about his going with her, or did she intend to go home at all?

She touched his arm, and he lifted his head. "You have my word, I'm not trying to ditch you," she said, apparently reading his mind. "It's just that while I was packing this afternoon, I suddenly remembered I'd committed myself for the next month." She smiled crookedly. "We'll find Podly, I promise. And who knows, maybe Max and Tigger will come in handy. They're both hunting breeds; they can sniff out the satellite for us."

Luke laced his fingers through hers. "If you're really not trying to ditch me, then why do I have to go back to the hotel until Tuesday?"

Her cheeks turned a lovely pink, and her gaze dropped. She tried to pull away, but Luke actually tossed her hand away with a snort. "You're out of here ten minutes after I leave. Only you're not going home, you're running away again."

"That's not true! It's just that . . . I don't want . . . Dammit, I'm not going to be fit company for the next two days! I just want to be left alone, okay? Come back Tuesday afternoon, and we'll leave after supper."

"Not fit . . . What in hell are you talking about?"

Her cheeks turned blistering red. "Look, I started my period today, okay? And for the next two days, I'm going to be a miserable, achy grump."

He was so relieved, he started laughing.

Camry jumped up and ran out of the room.

Luke instantly sobered. "Hey, wait! I'm sorry!" he called, scrambling after her.

Her bedroom door nearly hit him when she slammed it shut, and she managed to get it locked before he could open it.

He thunked his head against it with a groan. "Camry, I'm sorry. I wasn't laughing at you. I mean, not really. Dammit, don't shut me out."

"Go away," she said, her voice coming through the wood only inches from his. "I'll be right here come Tuesday, I promise."

God, he was an idiot. For a man who'd managed to earn several degrees, he didn't seem to have a clue when it came to women. Which was surprising, considering he'd spent the first thirteen years of his life in an all-female household.

"Have I mentioned that I was raised by my single mother, my grandmother, and my aunt?" he asked, his head still resting on the door.

"No," she whispered after several heartbeats.

"And I can certainly attest the old myth is true, that when women live together their menses gravitate to the same schedule." He chuckled.

"What's so funny about that?" she growled.

"I just thought of your poor father, living in a household of eight women."

"That's a sexist remark!"

"It's not sexist if it's a scientific fact."

"Go away, Luke."

He straightened away from the door, running his fingers through his hair. Dammit to hell. He didn't want to leave. "The only reason I pointed out my having been raised by women was to let you know that I don't care how grumpy you get. I can pretty much handle anything you dish out." He hesitated. "Except being told to get lost."

When she didn't respond, Luke walked to the living room, threw himself down on the couch, and glared at the transmitter sitting on the coffee table. He leaned forward and picked up the stubbornly silent instrument. "You are obviously the design of a feminine mind," he muttered. "Why in hell do women have to be so complicated?"

"Because it's our job."

Luke jumped, fumbling to hold on to the transmitter, but it still went flying when Camry plopped down on the couch beside him.

"Because men are such simple creatures, women need to be complicated to balance things out," she continued, preventing him from going after the transmitter by snuggling against his chest.

Luke wrapped his arms around her and sighed heavily.

"Did your mother really tell you to get lost all the time?"

"No, my aunt did. She was a grumpy woman every day, but it wasn't until I was nine or ten that I realized she was downright mean a few days each month." He softly snorted. "The day we moved out of Gram's house and in with my new stepfather, my mother actually apologized for making me live with Aunt Faith for thirteen years."

"Why was Aunt Faith so grumpy?"

"Who knows. My guess is she was bitter. Even though my biological father took off the day he found out about me, I think Faith was jealous that Mom had even had a passionate affair." He shrugged. "Faith didn't have much luck with men, and I finally decided she was lonely."

"Maybe she would have had better luck if she wasn't so grumpy."

Luke chuckled humorlessly. "I actually told her that once. It was around the time my mother met André Renoir. I was eleven. Aunt Faith went from grumpy to openly hostile the deeper in love Mom fell with André."

Camry popped her head up. "André Renoir became your stepfather?"

Luke nodded. "When I was thirteen. And he legally adopted me the day they got married." He nudged her head to his chest so she'd quit looking at him. "I hadn't minded André up until then, since he made Mom happy. But I didn't see why I suddenly had to change my name, too, as well as let him have any say over my life."

She popped her head up again. "Was he mean to you?"

"Oh no. André is a good man, and he was sincerely interested in me," he said, pulling her back against him. "But for the first thirteen years of my life, I pretty much did what I wanted without receiving much flack. I'd lock myself in my room for days with my books and computer, and nobody bothered me. But after we moved in with André, the man kept dragging me outdoors, saying I needed to get the stink blown off me."

Luke laughed. "He tried to teach me to play baseball, but I kept striking out on purpose. So he took me hunting with him, and I made enough noise stomping through the woods to scare off all the game. But God bless the patient man, no matter how much I sabotaged his good intentions, he just kept trying . . . until the day I ran away from home."

"You ran away from home? How old were you?"

"Fourteen. My mother and André told me I was going to have a baby sister." He chuckled. "Even though I knew all about the birds and bees, I was horrified to suddenly realize they'd been having *sex*. I waited until they went to bed that night, then took off."

"Where'd you go?" she asked with a giggle.

"I decided to go back and live with Gram and Aunt Faith, so I started walking to Vancouver, which was a little over a hundred miles away. But I didn't care. I just wanted my old self-centered life back, grumpy aunt and all."

"And? Did they take you back?"

"I didn't make it ten miles. It was the dead of winter, and André found me half frozen to death, stubbornly trudging along the side of the road.

He never said a word the entire ride back home. But when we drove into our dooryard, instead of letting me go inside and warm up, he dragged me out to the woodshed, and—"

"He *beat* you?" she gasped as she straightened.

Luke grinned at her fierce expression. "No. But it was the first time I'd ever seen him angry. He handed me a crosscut saw and axe, and told me to start working up next year's firewood. And that while I did, I was to contemplate one simple question, and give him the answer when I was done."

"And that question was?"

"He asked me the definition of love."

Camry's eyes grew huge with anticipation. "And what did you tell him love was?"

Luke snorted. "I was fourteen—what in hell did I know about love?"

She scrambled off the couch and stood glaring at him. "But you had to have told him something! You obviously didn't freeze to death in the wood-shed."

Luke stood, then walked over and picked up the transmitter before looking at her again. "Oh, I came up with an answer that at least got me back in the house—though it didn't get me out of working up eight cords of firewood. André told me what I'd come up with was only a start, but that he would know I had figured out the rest when I finally apologized to my mother."

"And did you?"

He nodded. "When I was twenty."

"So, what's the definition of love?" she asked, her expression eager again.

Luke eyed her speculatively, wondering how far he could push her. "If you let me stay, I'll tell you on the drive to Pine Creek."

She actually stomped her foot in frustration, then immediately grabbed her leg and hopped back to the couch. "Now look what you made me do," she muttered, lifting her foot onto the coffee table as she glared up at him. "That's blackmail."

"You can thank your mother for teaching me that one." He sat down on the table, tossed the transmitter on her lap, and set her foot on his thigh so he could take off her sock and rub her ankle. "When I came out of the woodshed, I told André that love meant not hurting someone who loved me."

She leaned back and started toying with the transmitter. "That was a good answer for a fourteen-year-old kid."

"But incomplete, according to André."

"Why didn't he just tell you the whole answer?"

"Don't think I didn't ask him to. But he said it's

not something one person can explain to another; I had to *feel* love to know it."

She suddenly smiled. "Then you can't tell me, either, which means you just gave up your chance to blackmail me into staying."

He arched a brow. "Or I just made you curious enough to let me stay."

"How do you figure that?"

"I told you that I apologized to my mother when I was twenty. Aren't you even a little bit curious as to why then?"

She looked down at the transmitter, shrugging indifferently. "Maybe."

But Luke knew she was dying to know—likely wondering if some girl had broken his heart. "Can I stay?" he asked softly.

She looked up, the gleam of challenge in her eyes. "Only if you give me a hint as to what happened when you were twenty that led you to have your great epiphany."

Oh yeah, he had her now—he just had to reel her in. Luke stared off over her head as if considering her offer, then finally locked his gaze on hers. "I died."

Chapter Eleven

Camry pulled out of the L.L.Bean parking lot in Freeport late Tuesday afternoon, her partner in crime sitting beside her, two dogs and all their paraphernalia in the rear seat, and the back of her SUV crammed full of cold-weather camping equipment and supplies.

Luke immediately became engrossed in the new and supposedly improved GPS tracking device he'd just purchased, and Camry turned north onto Interstate 95 with a smile of anticipation. As much as she loved her doggie friends and tending bar at Dave's, she realized there was nothing like a winter camping trip to blow off the cobwebs—and a dream guy who just happened to be in lust with her to add a bit of interest.

Cam thought back to all the boyfriends she'd had over the years, and tried to decide if she had spent time with any of them that even came close to the weekend she'd just spent with Luke. The last three days had been amazingly intimate—which Cam found rather interesting, since she had always equated intimacy with lovemaking. But she'd shared her bed with Luke for three wonderfully celibate nights, and she couldn't remember the last time she'd slept so soundly.

Cam merged into traffic with a silent giggle, remembering what had happened Sunday morning. Since Fiona had blown his cover, Lucian Renoir the physicist had suddenly emerged, and Luke had risen long before sunrise, dug out his laptop, and started crunching numbers. When she'd run into the living room in her pajamas, frantic that *he* had suddenly decided to ditch *her,* she'd found him writing on one of her walls.

Apparently so engrossed in his work that he wasn't even aware he was using her wall as a whiteboard, Luke had appeared confused when she'd shouted. He'd apologized profusely as he went to the kitchen to get a wet rag, but then *he* had shouted when he'd returned to find her overwriting one of his equations. They'd spent the rest of the day covering two more walls with equations as they retraced Podly's solstice descent—a trajectory that defied every law of physics. And not only had Camry not bothered to change out of her pajamas, she had completely forgotten to be grumpy and miserable.

She was still a bit shaken by how quickly Luke had figured out her little game of letting her boyfriends think they were having mind-blowing sex. Hell, she'd gotten so good at it, she had practically convinced herself that she was utterly, totally fulfilled.

The men certainly had never complained.

Except Luke: after only two days, he'd wanted to wring her neck. She still couldn't believe he'd actually pulled out a condom, opened the damn thing, and then asked if she knew what it was. She should have been outraged, but instead she had found herself wondering what he planned to do about her . . . virginity. Would he continue their lusty little affair on her terms, or did he see her as a challenge now? Did he have hopes of taking things to the next level?

She wasn't worried he'd push her into going all the way; Luke didn't seem to have a pushy bone in his body. Camry smiled at the road ahead. He certainly would try nudging her, though, because for all of his civilized trappings, he was still a perfectly functioning male.

But then, she also loved a good challenge.

"According to my GPS, we're going seventy-six miles per hour," he said into the silence, glancing over at the odometer.

Camry kept her foot steady on the accelerator. "I'm just keeping up with what little traffic there is."

A moan came from the backseat, and Luke glanced over his shoulder. "Um . . . Max doesn't look so good. He's drooling, and his eyes are watery."

"He gets carsick. The pill I gave him in Freeport will kick in soon."

"You intend to keep him drugged the entire trip?"

"Max won't need his medicine once he gets in the snowcat; he'll be too excited about being on an adventure. He only gets sick in cars because he worries he might be going to the vet."

Luke started pushing buttons on his GPS again.

Camry swiped it out of his hand and set it on the dash on her side of the truck, out of his reach. "Okay. I didn't make you go back to your hotel, and we're on the road. So pony up, Dr. Renoir. If you died when you were twenty, how come you're still breathing?"

"Because the raging river that killed me also slammed me into a rock and knocked the air back into my lungs."

She scowled over at him. "From the beginning, Luke. And your intriguing little story had better explain what made you apologize to your mother."

He started repacking everything that had come with the GPS. "You already know I have a kid sister named Kate. Well, when she was five, Mom and André and I took her to the pound on Christmas Eve, and she picked out a monster of a dog that appeared to be eight or nine years old. He was coal black with wiry hair, half of one of his ears was missing, and his eyes were clouded with developing cataracts. I tried to get her to choose one of the puppies, or at least something less pathetic-looking, but Kate claimed she wanted that one because it was the beautifulest dog in the world and she was going to love it forever."

He shrugged. "She insisted on naming it Maxine, even though I explained it was a male dog. But on Christmas morning, when Kate took Maxine out to play, almost two hours went by before anyone realized they weren't in the yard."

"Two hours?"

"It was one of those 'I thought she was with you' things. Mom thought Kate had ridden over to check on our neighbor with André, and André had driven away thinking she was in the house playing with the toys Santa had brought her."

He leaned his head back and closed his eyes, and Camry realized that even though he'd promised to tell her his story, it obviously wasn't going to be easy for him.

"When André got back and Mom realized Kate wasn't with him, we all started looking for her. When we hadn't found her an hour later, we went back to the house and Mom called our local conservation officer to start an organized search. André and I put on snowshoes and split up, and started searching in opposite directions."

"But if you needed snowshoes, didn't Kate and the dog leave tracks you could follow?" Cam whispered, suddenly afraid this wasn't going to be any easier for her to hear than it was for him to tell.

He glanced over at her, then looked out his side window at the darkened woods passing by. "We'd had an ice storm two days before, and Kate and Maxine were light enough that they could walk on the crust, whereas André and I kept breaking through. We eventually moved far enough away from each other that I could no longer hear him calling for Kate. But I could hear the distant roar of the river." He hesitated, then said softly, "That's when I stepped under a giant spruce tree that had sheltered the snow from the rain, and found the tracks of a small child and dog."

He looked out the windshield, but Cam knew he wasn't seeing the road. "I started running in the direction the tracks went, which was straight toward the river."

Camry tightened her grip on the steering wheel. "I know Kate survived, because you said she's Fiona's age. So I don't want to hear any more of this story, Luke."

"Yes, you do." He reached over and patted her thigh. "Because this is when I learned exactly what I had put my mother through when I'd run away six years earlier." He took a deep breath, but left his hand on her leg. "I had never before and have never since been so scared. I broke into a cold sweat, having horrific images of Kate being swept away by the river. I hated that damn dog for luring her into the woods, and swore that when I found them I would wring his ugly black neck."

His hand on her thigh tightened, then was suddenly gone. "I still have nightmares about what I saw when I reached the river. Kate was dangling on the edge of the ice only a few feet above the rushing water. She was utterly motionless, and

that dog—that beautiful, mangy pound mutt—
had his teeth clamped on her coat, holding her
back from falling in." Luke looked over at her. "I
have no idea how long Maxine had been holding
her like that, but I swear that if Kate fell, he had
every intention of going with her."

Camry checked her mirror and guided her
truck to the side of the interstate, braking to a
stop all the way over on the grass before shutting
off the engine. She closed her eyes and buried her
face in her hands on the steering wheel.

"Hey, it's okay," he said, cupping her head in
his broad palm. "I stripped off my snowshoes and
carefully made my way to them. Maxine was quivering uncontrollably, and his mouth was bloody
from the strain on his teeth. His feet were bloody,
too, and I could see where he'd been gouging the
crust, trying to pull Kate up over the lip of ice."

Picturing the scene all too vividly in her mind,
and fearing what was coming, Camry scrambled
over the console and into his arms.

Luke cradled her against his chest and quietly
continued. "As I approached them, I felt the ice
shelf start to buckle. Just then I heard several
shouts, and realized that André and some other
men had spotted us. But it was too late. I grabbed
Kate's coat and pulled her up, yanking her out of
Maxine's mouth, then flung her as far as I could

back across the crust just as the shelf gave way. The dog and I fell into the river."

"Oh, God," Camry whispered. "The water must have been freezing."

"It literally took my breath away. The force of the rapids slammed me into boulders and held me under until I thought my lungs were going to burst."

"And y-you died."

His arms around her tightened. "I suddenly wasn't cold anymore, and everything went . . . peaceful."

"But then you came back."

"The current must have slammed me into another rock, and I broke the surface and sucked air back into my lungs. But I was completely disoriented. Then something snagged the shoulder of my jacket, and I felt clawing on my legs."

"Maxine."

"Just like with Kate, that damn dog latched on to me and started swimming across the current. There was enough light left that I could see the river was frozen solid where it turned to flat water up ahead, and I knew that if we didn't make it to shore, we were going to be swept under the ice."

"You both made it."

"I did."

"A-and Maxine?"

"I spent the next three weeks searching for his body, but I never found him."

"He died!" Cam wailed, burying her face in his shirt. She punched his arm. "I said I didn't want to hear this story!"

"I've never told anyone what happened after I fell in the river; not about my drowning, nor what Maxine had done," Luke murmured into her hair.

That surprised her. "But why? Wouldn't you at least want Kate to know that Maxine died saving your life?"

"It seemed too personal to share with anyone. Or maybe . . . sacred is a better word. So I just let everyone be thankful that Maxine had saved Kate's life." He sighed heavily. "The dog hadn't lured her into the woods; he had followed her."

Cam relaxed against him. She was still upset that Maxine hadn't survived, but damned glad that Luke had. "Did you find out why Kate had left the dooryard?"

"She told us she was looking for a special rock in the pool of pretty pebbles she remembered seeing that summer, when she and André had been fishing in the river."

"What made her think she could find it with snow on the ground?"

"Five-year-olds don't think about silly details like that; they just go after what they want." His lips touched her hair again. "All Kate was focused on was finding a special rock so she could give it to me for Christmas. Because, she told me that night when she came to my room after we got back from the hospital, she didn't want me returning to college without something to remind me of home . . . and of her."

He took a ragged breath. "I came unglued. She'd nearly died trying to find some stupid rock for me, and I started yelling at her. But instead of bursting into tears like a normal kid, you know what she did?"

Camry said nothing, because she couldn't.

"She wrapped her tiny arms around my legs and told me that she loved me so much, her heart hurt when she thought of my missing her the way she missed me." He took another shuddering breath. "And then she explained that she could sit in my room whenever she missed me, but that I didn't have anything to remind me of her when I was away at college."

"My knees buckled," he continued, his voice raspy, "and I knelt down to hug her. But before I could, Kate held up her tiny fist and opened her fingers to reveal a black-and-white speckled pebble in her palm. She told me it was a lot smaller than the rock she'd wanted to find for me, but that she'd been forced to grab the beautifulest

one she could reach in the pool of open water, because Maxine had kept pulling on her coat."

Luke ducked his head to press his cheek
against hers. "You know what love really is,
Camry? It's uncompromising, unpretentious, and
unconditional, and sometimes it makes your heart
hurt. I apologized to Kate for yelling at her, and
she patted my cheek and said that she knew I was
angry because I loved her—just like Maxine had
growled at her when she'd climbed down to the
water. Kate said, and I quote, 'Maxine didn't let
me fall in the river because he knew I was going
to love him forever.' "

Luke rested his chin on her head with a sigh.
"I had never paid much attention to Kate for the
first five years of her life. I didn't have a clue what
to do with an infant, and by the time she was a
toddler, I was away at college most of the year
or working in town and hanging out with my
friends all summer. But that didn't stop her from
loving me so much that her heart hurt when I was
gone."

He lifted Cam's chin to make her look at him,
his smile tender in the glow of the dash lights. "I
tucked Kate in bed, then went downstairs to the
living room, got down on my knees, and apologized to my mother for running away when I was
fourteen. Then I apologized to André for being

such a self-centered bastard, and thanked him for not giving up on me."

He shifted beneath her without breaking his embrace, then pressed something into the palm of her hand. "Here. If you try real hard, I bet you can feel the love, too," he whispered, folding her fingers over the tiny, smooth object. "The next summer, just before I headed off to college again, I took Kate down to the river and we built a huge rock cairn in honor of Maxine. Then I searched until I found a very special rock, and gave it to Kate. She hugged it to her heart and said it was the beautifulest rock she'd ever seen." He squeezed Cam's fist. "I've carried this pebble since that Christmas. No matter where I am in the world, or what I'm doing, I just have to reach in my pocket to know that I am uncompromisingly, unpretentiously, and unconditionally loved."

He lifted her hand to his mouth and kissed it. "And the moral of my story, I've since realized, is that sometimes our most profound lessons come from a five-year-old child, and sometimes they show up as a mangy old dog."

"Or as a fellow scientist who for some reason has clamped his teeth into me, and refuses to let go until I go home and apologize to my mother?"

He suddenly stiffened. "No," he said with a growl. He set her back over the console and into her seat. "*Don't* compare me to Maxine. That dog was a gutsy, selfless hero, whereas I'm a self-serving bastard who didn't think twice about stealing someone's life's work."

She gasped softly. "Is that how you see yourself?"

He looked over at her, the dash lights accentuating the harsh planes of his face. "Fiona had it wrong, Camry. I'm nobody's miracle."

"But you didn't mean to destroy Podly."

"I sure as hell meant to use the data I was trying to download," he said, turning away to look out his side window.

Camry stared out the windshield, desperately wanting to tell Luke that *he* hadn't caused Podly to crash, Fiona had. But even though she knew they would have to talk about it eventually, she simply didn't have the courage to open that particular Pandora's box quite yet.

She started the truck, checked for oncoming traffic, and accelerated back onto the interstate. Maybe Fiona did have it wrong. Miracles were the stuff of magic, after all, and the magic wasn't known for rewarding hijackers and no-good, rotten liars. It was more prone to toying with them the way a cat toyed with a mouse—or the way an impish niece with a thing for satellites did—just before sending down some seriously bad karma.

Yeah, well . . . if she and Luke had some dues to pay, Camry couldn't think of a better person to pay them with. Because contrary to what he might think of himself, she knew that, just like Maxine, Lucian Renoir had no intention of letting the raging river sweep her away.

Chapter Twelve

They arrived in Pine Creek shortly after midnight, but it took them another two hours to get their hands on a snowcat—which they virtually stole out from under the noses of the TarStone Mountain Ski Resort night-grooming crew. It was nearly three in the morning before they got back to the truck they'd hidden several miles from the resort, and Luke couldn't decide if Camry had a death wish or if she just got her jollies from skulking around in the shadows.

He did learn some interesting things about himself, however. One, he probably should stick to physics, as he'd likely starve to death if he had to steal for a living; and two, even if he had spent the entire night in a cold sweat, he rather liked performing any number of illegal acts with Camry. At one point he'd even been tempted to look down the front of *her* pants to see what equipment *she* was packing; the woman appeared to have nerves of steel, the focus of a Navy Seal, and the mind of a master criminal.

She also had a rather perverse sense of timing; like when they'd been hiding in the maintenance garage while they'd waited for one of the workers to kindly refuel the groomer they intended to . . . borrow. Apparently having grown bored, Camry had gone after *Luke's* package. But just as he'd been trying to wrestle her hands away from his belt buckle, the garage lights had suddenly gone out and the man had left.

Camry had immediately returned to criminal mode, leaving Luke—and his bewildered lower brain—sprawled in the corner, in total darkness, wondering when exactly he had lost his mind.

Camry finally pulled the snowcat to a stop beside her SUV and shut off the engine, snapped on the interior lights, and shot him a smug smile.

Luke pried his fingers off the handle he'd been

clutching in a death grip. "Would you care to explain what your intentions were back there in the garage?"

"I intended to steal us transportation. Which I did."

"No, I mean when we were stuck hiding behind that equipment. It wasn't exactly the time or place for slap and tickle. And besides, I thought you were . . . um, off the market for a few days."

Her smile turned downright cheeky. "Hey, just because the Ferris wheel isn't running doesn't mean the *entire* amusement park is shut down," she said with a laugh, opening her door and hopping out.

Luke stared after her, nonplussed.

He suddenly gave a bark of laughter and scrambled after her, happy to realize their little affair was still on—which made him glad he'd snuck out to the drugstore yesterday and purchased a whole box of condoms.

Camry opened the back door of the truck to let the dogs out as Luke approached her, still chuckling. "What's so funny?" she asked.

"Oh, nothing. I was just thinking how this excursion into the wilderness is going to be a lot more interesting than my last one."

Tigger bounded out of the truck behind

Max, only to give a yelp of surprise when she suddenly disappeared. Luke fished the dachshund out of the snow and set her back on the seat. "Yes, Tigger," he said, brushing off the shivering dog. "I'll bet this is exactly how you pictured your Christmas sleepover with Auntie Cam, isn't it?"

"Her sweater is in the green backpack," Camry said. She opened the rear hatch and started transferring their gear to the snowcat. "Just stomp down a circle in the snow so she can go pee."

Luke dug through the backpack, found what looked like a doll's sweater, and started dressing Tigger. Or he tried to, realizing he should have paid better attention when Kate had conned him into playing house with her dolls. "At least it's bright pink, so we'll be able to find you," he muttered, pushing what he hoped was the neck down over Tigger's head. "What are we going to do for fuel?" he called back to Camry. "I don't remember seeing any gas stations on Springy when I was there."

"I stole this particular groomer because it burns diesel. And Megan and Jack are building a camp on the lake at the base of the mountain, which means they would have lugged up a drum of fuel last summer that we can use."

"Did you hear that, Tig? We're going to teach you to steal, too. That way we can all share a jail cell so you won't be scarred for life."

Luke finally sighed in defeat, scooped Tigger up, and carried her to the back of the truck. "Here," he said, holding the dog out to Camry. "You figure this contraption out and I'll load our gear."

She tucked her hands behind her back. "You need the practice for when you have kids," she said, her eyes shining with amusement.

Luke hugged the half-dressed dachshund to his chest. "I've decided not to have children, because I'm afraid they might addle my brain."

Camry instantly sobered, spun around, grabbed their sleeping bags, and headed to the snowcat.

Luke smiled at her stomping away, and rubbed Tigger's head with the short beard he'd started growing three days ago for their camping trip.

Oh yeah, it was going to be a very interesting adventure.

Camry gritted her teeth as she grabbed the handle to keep herself from flying into the windshield, rethinking her brilliant idea of teaching Luke how to drive the snowcat. "Are you *aiming* for every damn rock and fallen log?"

"It's not like they're marked with BUMP signs." He shoved Max into the backseat. "I can't see them because Max keeps breathing on the glass and fogging it up."

"Wait. Stop here," she said. "I think this is the turnoff we need to take."

"You *think*?"

Cam scowled over at him. "It's been years since I've been this far north. I'll get my bearings once the sun rises." She reached over and shut off the engine, opened her door, then nearly fell out when Max shoved past her. "Okay, you over-grown brat, it's time we set down some rules," she said, lunging after the dog. She took hold of the lab's head and held him facing her, her nose only inches from his. "One, you wait until I tell you it's okay to get out. And two, you stay in the backseat with Tigger. You try to crawl in the front with us again, and you're riding on the roof with our gear."

"That put the fear of God in him," Luke said, walking around the snowcat with Tigger in his arms. He stopped to look at their surround-ings in the stingy light of the breaking dawn. "It might have been years since you've been up here, but I just spent two months scouring these woods. This tote road leads up the south side of Springy." He pointed in the other direction.

"And that way will take us closer to the lake, and eventually around to the north side of the mountain."

"Then we should go that way," she said. "Since your trajectory data points to the satellite's having come in from the north."

"Except that it couldn't have," he contradicted. "Based on its orbit at the time it malfunctioned, Podly should have crashed into the south side of Springy."

Cam stopped packing down the snow to make a spot for Tigger and looked at him. "So are you suggesting we search the same woods you already spent two months searching, or do you want to look where the satellite really is? Because I happen to know it's on the north side of the mountain."

He narrowed his eyes at her. "How?"

"Because I watched its entire descent."

"You actually *saw* it?"

Cam took Tigger out of his arms and set the dachshund in the circle she'd stomped down. "Winter was having her baby right then, and my other sisters and I were sitting down on the dock in front of her home, waiting for the big arrival. That's when we noticed what we thought was a meteor streaking through the sky, heading right toward Springy Mountain. It was coming from the north, traveling south. We all saw it, but just then Mom came out of the house and shouted to us that we had a brand-new baby niece." She shrugged. "I completely forgot about it until Saturday, when you told me Podly had crashed north of Pine Creek last June."

Luke stared at her, his jaw slack. "Then I guess we head north, don't we? Wait. You said you were at Winter's house. She had her baby at home?"

Cam nodded. "My mother and all my sisters had their babies at home. It's sort of a MacKeage tradition."

His jaw went slack again.

"What's so odd about that?" she asked. "Women have been having babies at home since we lived in caves."

"But what if something went wrong? You're miles from the nearest hospital."

Seeing that Tigger was done with her business, Cam set her in the snowcat, then turned back to Luke. "I guess you could say that it's also our tradition to have relatively easy births."

Luke's expression turned unreadable. "So if you were to have a baby . . . would you be expected to have it at home, too?"

"Expected? No. Each of my sisters chose to have her babies at home with a midwife, but they weren't *expected* to. In fact, Daddy practically begged them to go to the hospital." She started looking around for Max. "But if I ever do decide to have children, I would likely follow tradition."

Luke took hold of her sleeve and turned her to face him. "Does that scare you?"

"It's a moot point, since I'm not having kids."

"Because they'll steal your passion for science?" he asked softly.

"And because I want it to be my choice, not the universe's."

"Excuse me?"

Camry eyed him for several heartbeats, then sat down on the track of the snowcat with a sigh. "Okay, since you're madly in lust with me, I suppose you have a right to know why I've been . . . reluctant to have intercourse."

He snorted, but then held up his hand when she shot him a scowl. "Okay, we'll go with *reluctant*." He sat down beside her. "So what's the universe got to do with your having sex?"

Cam hesitated, wondering just how much of her family background she should disclose. But the more time she spent with Luke, the more she realized he wasn't at all like any of the men she'd dated. He was . . .

Hell. For the first time in her life, she was tempted to risk it all on a man.

And since he would be risking it all, too, he

certainly deserved to know what he was getting himself into, didn't he?

She pivoted to face him, made several attempts to start, then finally said, "Have you ever heard the saying that the seventh son of a seventh son is gifted?"

He arched a brow. "I believe I've heard something to that effect."

"Well, my mother was supposed to be the seventh son of a seventh son, but when she was born a *girl,* everyone thought that was the end of that. But instead of the end, Grace Sutter's birth was actually the beginning of an even stranger axiom. You see, Mom and her six brothers, and her sister Mary, were all born on the summer solstice."

He leaned away, both eyebrows raised in disbelief. "All eight kids?"

She nodded. "But here's where it gets even more improbable. Mom had seven daughters, and all of us were born on the *winter* solstice."

Luke snorted. "Now you're just messing with me."

Cam took hold of his sleeve and looked him directly in the eye, letting him see she was deadly serious. "My sisters' children have been born on random dates throughout the years, all except for Fiona, who was born on this summer's solstice. And Winter is Mom's seventh daughter."

"It's just a date on a calendar, Camry. Millions of kids have been born on one of the solstices. But what does any of that have to do with your reluctance to have sex?"

"Well, there's another tradition in our family," she said, dropping her gaze and letting go of his sleeve. "It seems that all six of my sisters got pregnant the very first time they made love to their husbands," she whispered.

He said nothing for several heartbeats, then softly asked, "And were they all virgins when they met their husbands?"

"No. Or at least several of them weren't." She stared off into the woods. "I believe Winter was. Heather got married when she was eighteen, so she might have been, too. But I'm pretty sure Megan, Sarah, Chelsea, and Elizabeth weren't." She looked over at Luke. "But their virginity is not the issue. Every one of them got pregnant the very first time they made love to the man they eventually *married*."

"And so you've never gone all the way because you've been afraid that . . . what? That you might get pregnant and then have to marry the father? But birth control is very reliable today."

"That's what Megan and Sarah and Elizabeth thought. I know that Sarah was on birth control pills, and Megan told me Jack used a condom. But don't you see? It's like the *universe* picked out their husbands for them."

"They didn't have to marry those men, Camry. That was their choice."

"But they loved them."

"Then what's the problem? Everything worked out for the best."

She stood up, crossing her arms to hug herself as she faced the woods. "But what if I want to love someone and not have babies with him?" She spun around to face him. "Where is it written that I can't have one without the other?"

He walked over and cupped her face, rubbing his thumbs across her cheek, and Cam was startled to realize she was crying.

He pressed his lips to her forehead, then pulled her into his arms and held her against his chest. "It isn't written anywhere, Camry. If you ever decide to get married, it will be to the man *you* choose, not who the universe chooses. And if you have a baby with him, it will be the choice of both of you."

"But I want to make love to you," she whispered.

He tilted her head back and looked down at her in surprise. "You do?" He grinned somewhat drunkenly. "You've fallen in lust with me?"

She buried her face in his chest again. "I don't know what I'm feeling," she growled. "Other than confused. What if we make love and I get pregnant?"

"You won't. We'll take precautions."

Cam melted against him with a heavy sigh. "Father Daar says that if a baby's wanting to be born, no contraceptive will stop it."

"Father Daar?"

She looked up at him. "He's an old priest who used to live in a cabin up on TarStone, but now he lives on the coast with Matt's brother, Kenzie Gregor. Daar's been around forever, and presided over my parents' and all of my sisters' weddings. And he's always told us girls that if a child is wanting to be born, it will be, and that we just have to accept what *Providence* decides."

Luke gave her a crooked smile. "Please don't take this the wrong way, but for a scientist, you have some really strange notions."

She nestled back against him. "I can't help it," she said with another sigh. "I was born into a really strange family." She looked up at him. "So . . . are you still in lust with me? Or have I managed to scare you off?"

He arched a brow. "That would depend on if your father is going to come after me with a shotgun. Greylen strikes me as rather old-fashioned." He grinned. "Is that the real reason your sisters married the men who got them pregnant?"

Cam toyed with the zipper on his jacket. "And if Daddy did come after you with a shotgun," she asked, finally looking up into his eyes, "would you make an honest woman of me, or jump on the first plane back to France?"

"Hmmm . . . I don't know."

Cam squirmed to break free, but Luke pulled her back against him with a laugh, and tucked her head under his chin. "Give me a minute here, MacKeage. On the one hand, I'm no more ready than you are to think about having a baby, but . . ." He ducked his head to look her in the eye. "But the more time we spend together, the more in lust with you I get. And I do have a whole box of condoms that I'd hate to see go to waste. But then . . ." He suddenly set her away, shaking his head. "Nope, I'm too tired right now to know what I'd do. So let's head north, find a place to set up camp, and have a nap." He spun around and headed into the woods in the direction Max had gone. "Don't worry, you'll be the first to know what I decide," he said over his shoulder.

Cam stood gaping at him walking away. Of all the . . .

Wait. Had he been *teasing* her?

But nobody teased her. Ever. They didn't dare, because they knew that though she occasionally got mad, she *always* got even.

Cam suddenly smiled. So he wanted to have a nap, did he?

She just as suddenly scowled.

He'd brought a *whole box* of condoms?

Chapter Thirteen

$\mathcal{B}$y the time they finished setting up camp halfway up the north side of Springy Mountain—after stopping at Megan and Jack's building lot to refuel the snowcat—Camry was so exhausted that she didn't care if she *died* a virgin; she simply didn't have the energy to get even with Luke.

The dogs cooperated, and immediately settled down on their new doggie bed inside the large tent she and Luke had just pitched. Getting Luke to cooperate, however, was another matter entirely, as the man appeared jumpier than a cat in a room full of rocking chairs.

"I told you those PowerBars were loaded with

sugar and caffeine," she muttered, stripping off her outer clothes.

He looked up from unlacing his boots. "We'd be camping in a snowbank right now if I hadn't eaten them," he said, waving at the tent they were in. "I've been awake for over thirty hours."

Stripped down to her long johns, Cam crawled into the sleeping bags she'd zipped together. "If you'd taken a nap like I did yesterday, instead of sneaking out to buy condoms, you wouldn't have needed to eat them. Now you won't be able to sleep."

"Oh, I'll sleep, all right," he said, crawling in beside her.

Luke then let out a yawn—which made her yawn—and folded his hands on his stomach. But instead of falling asleep, Camry noticed he started twiddling his thumbs as he stared up at the tent roof. "You do realize that as soon as your father discovers one of his groomers is missing, he's going to know you're the one who stole it."

"I know."

"Which will lead your mother to believe that you'll be home for Christmas."

"Go to sleep, Luke."

He stayed silent for all of sixty seconds. "Only Grace didn't seem to be worried about Christmas," he murmured, apparently talking to himself as much as to her. "She asked me to have you home by the *solstice.*"

Even though her eyes were closed, she could tell that his thumbs had stopped twiddling and that he was looking at her. "I thought it was strange at the time, but now I know it's because it's your birthday." He snorted. "As well as all your sisters' birthday."

"Go to *sleep,* Luke."

A full ninety seconds went by before she felt him roll toward her. "And since your big day is December twentieth, I've been thinking maybe we could hop on a plane after your birthday party and spend Christmas with my family in British Columbia."

That got her eyes open. "What?"

Propping his head on his hand as he faced her, he rested his other hand across her belly to cup her opposite hip. "It'll be fun," he said with an eager smile. "Mom and André are dying to meet you, and Kate is beside herself with curiosity. She's been sending me at least ten text messages a day for the last week, asking about you."

"You *told* your family about me?"

"Of course. And I promised that I'd bring you home to meet them."

"But why?" Cam whispered, horrified at the thought of meeting his family, considering she couldn't even face her own. "What did you tell them about me?"

He suddenly flopped onto his back, folded his hands on his belly, and stared up at the tent roof again. "I told them that just as soon as I worked up the nerve, I was going to ask you to marry me."

Camry bolted upright. "You *what!*" she attempted to shout—only it came out as a squeak.

He hadn't really just mentioned the M-word, had he?

He also sat up, and took her suddenly trembling hands in his. "I was going to wait until after we found Podly and you made up with your parents to ask you." Two flags of red rose into his shadowy beard. "In fact, I even planned to buy a ring and get down on one knee, but . . ." He lifted her hands to his mouth and kissed them. "But when you told me about your strange family traditions yet admitted you wanted to make love to me anyway, I started thinking that maybe I should take blatant advantage of your confusion and propose *before* we made love."

He let go of her hands to close her gaping mouth, then immediately placed his finger over her lips to keep her from saying anything.

Not that she could have.

"I realize this is rather sudden for you, so I really don't want you to give me an answer right now."

"But you're only in *lust* with me," Cam managed to whisper behind his finger.

He reached down and took hold of her hands again. "Oh, I'm definitely in lust with you. But while we were hiding in the maintenance garage, I realized that lust doesn't hold a candle to the intimacy we've shared this past week." He took what appeared to be a fortifying breath and held her hands to his chest, over his solidly beating heart. "So, Camry MacKeage, would you do me the honor of *considering* spending the rest of your life being intimate with me?"

She dropped her gaze to her hands clasped in his. "I-I have to think about it."

He released what sounded like a relieved sigh and flopped back on the air mattress, pulling her with him and snuggling her up against his side. "Thank you. But while you're thinking, I'd like you to consider one more thing." He tilted her chin up for her to look at him. "Marrying me just might be your chance to trump the universe."

"How?"

"By your getting married *before* you make love to your husband. That way you can't ever question that you're the one doing the choosing, not Providence."

Cam tucked her head into his shoulder and stared across his chest. "But what if I marry you, then we make love, and I *don't* get pregnant?" she whispered, clutching his shirt in her fist. "That would mean you're *not* the man I'm supposed to marry."

His chest fell on a heavy sigh. "Camry, sweetheart, you have to stop letting your fear that something might or might not occur dictate your life. Your only basis for assuming that what happened to your sisters has any bearing on what will happen to you is your belief that *tradition* is even a tangible integer. But the very fact that your sisters loved the men they married precludes any direct correlation to their getting pregnant. If you were to develop a matrix, with tradition being X and seemingly related occurrences being Y, I believe you would see how rarely they actually intersect. In fact, I'd be surprised if such an equation could even be written, because—"

Camry stifled a yawn and melted bonelessly against him with deep and utter contentment. Because honest to God, the very fact that he was *lecturing* her made Cam's heart swell with the realization that he truly loved her!

And seeing how her ears weren't wanting to fall off, well . . . could that mean she just might love him back?

Chapter Fourteen

$\mathcal{S}$omewhere in the far reaches of sleep, Luke heard Max and Tigger stirring—only seconds before he heard the zipper on the tent slide open. The realization that it wasn't Camry doing the zipping, because she was snuggled tightly against him, made Luke bolt up in adrenaline-laced alarm.

"You people are trespassing," said the man holding the shotgun only inches from his chest, his voice a menacing growl.

Luke cut off Camry's yelp of surprise by shoving her behind his back when she also sprang upright. "We're not looking for trouble," he told the white-bearded, wild-haired old man. "We're just doing a little winter camping."

Camry peeked past Luke's arm. "You're the one trespassing," she said. "This mountain belongs to Jack and Megan Stone."

"You look like land developers to me," the man snarled, though he did lower the shotgun barrel slightly.

Which still disconcerted Luke, as now it was aimed at his groin. "We're not land developers," he said, leaning sideways to put himself in front of Camry again. He eyed Max and Tigger, wondering why neither dog seemed particularly worried. In fact, they looked downright pleased to have company. "We're on sabbatical from work, getting some fresh mountain air before we go home to our families for Christmas."

"I'm Camry MacKeage," Camry said, leaning around him again. "My family lives in Pine Creek. We own TarStone Mountain Ski Resort."

The gun barrel lowered several more inches as the man arched his bushy brows in surprise. "*Camry* MacKeage, you say?" His eyes narrowed again on Luke. "You Lucian Renoir?"

Luke stiffened. "Yes."

Their uninvited guest's expression suddenly turned eager. "Well okay, then!" he said, backing out of the tent—and taking his shotgun with him. Tigger and Max bounded after him. "I've been waiting weeks for you people to show up!" he continued from outside. "Dag-nab-it, it took you two long enough to get here!"

Luke turned to Camry with an inquisitive arch of his brow.

When she merely shrugged, they both scrambled to put on their boots. They slid their jackets on over their long johns and rushed for the tent door, but Luke pulled Camry to a stop. "Let me go first."

"It's obvious he's only a harmless old hermit."

"Who just happens to know our names? I spent two months on this mountain, and I never saw a trace of him. So just humor me, would you, and let me go out first?"

She stared into his eyes for what seemed like forever, then suddenly smiled and motioned toward the tent flap. "Be my guest, Maxine."

Luke shot her a warning scowl, then poked his head through the flap to find the man sitting on the ground, laughing uncontrollably as Tigger attacked his face with her tongue. Max was flopped on his back with all four paws in the air, his tail thumping the snow as the guy rubbed his belly. Luke looked around for the shotgun and saw it leaning against the track of the snowcat, beside the . . . next to the . . .

He scrambled out of the tent, pulling Camry with him. The moment she stood up, Luke surreptitiously motioned toward the cat. "Is that what I think it is?"

"Oh my God," she softly gasped. "That looks like Podly. Or at least its outer housing." She glanced briefly at the man, who seemed to have completely forgotten them in favor of playing with the dogs. "He's using our satellite as a *sled*?"

"You go check it out," Luke whispered, heading toward the man. He stopped and held his hand down to him. "You can call me Luke, Mr. . . . ?"

The still-laughing man took hold of Luke's hand, but instead of shaking it, he used it to pull himself to his feet. "Dag-nab-it, I seem to be getting older instead of younger," he chortled, finally shaking Luke's hand. "Name's Roger AuClair. You like that sled, Missy MacKeage? I'd be willing to sell it to you," he called to Camry. "Or if'n you want, I can custom make you one just like it, only out of wood scraps."

He walked over to her. "A wooden one would cost you less than this one, 'cause this stuff don't fall out of the sky every day, you know," he said, running his gnarled hand over the charred metal. "I still got to polish it up some. You got any sweets in your fancy snow machine?" he asked, peering in through the window of the snowcat. He looked back at Camry. "I'm open to bartering. Pound for pound, anything I build for you in exchange for anything you got that's sweet, be it home-baked or store-bought."

"I believe we have some sweet granola bars," Camry offered with obvious amusement. She glanced toward Luke, then down at the sled, then back at Roger. "But instead of trading me this beautiful piece, would you happen to have other parts of whatever fell out of the sky that we might barter for?"

"Something about this big, maybe?" Luke added, holding his hands not quite a foot apart. "Sort of square, and rather heavy for its size?"

"I might," Roger said, scratching his beard as his gaze moved to Luke. "You know anything about satellite dishes? 'Cause this thing," he muttered, kicking the sled, "knocked my television dish clean off my roof last June, just before it smashed into the trees behind my cabin. I fashioned another dish from the blasted thing's parts, but I only get half the channels I used to." His gaze narrowed. "I *might* be able to find something about the size you want, if'n you get all my channels to come in. As well as those sweet bar thingies your missy just mentioned."

"I know a little something about satellite dishes," Luke offered.

Roger snatched up his shotgun, grabbed the rope handle on his sled, and started off up the tote road they were camped beside. "Then come on, people! We only got two hours of daylight left. And today's Wednesday, and *Survivorman* is on tonight. I already missed nearly six months of episodes."

Luke stood beside Camry, both of them watching the man disappear around a curve, Max hot on his heels. Tigger, getting mired in the deep snow, rushed back to them and started whining.

Luke scooped up the dog. "Does AuClair look familiar to you?" he asked, still staring up the road. "Those green eyes of his, maybe?"

"I can't say," Camry murmured, "what with all that wild hair covering everything." She glanced up at Luke. "How does he know our names? And what did he mean, he's been waiting for us to show up for weeks?"

"I suppose we're going to have to ask him." Luke opened the door of the snowcat and set Tigger inside, then headed back to the tent. "Let's get dressed and secure everything here so we can catch up with him."

Luke crawled inside the tent, sat on the sleeping bag, and slipped off his boots to pull on his pants. "You know anything about television dishes?" he asked. "Because short of tying the old hermit up and ransacking his place—which, despite my actions to date, is one crime I refuse to consider—it looks as if we're going to have to repair his dish if we want Podly's data banks."

Camry fastened her pants, then slipped back into her boots. She reached over and shut off their catalytic heater, then quickly straightened their sleeping bags before heading back outside. "How many rocket scientists does it take to repair a television antenna?" she asked with a giggle.

"Two," Luke said, crawling out behind her. He pulled her into his arms and kissed the tip of her nose. "One to stand on the roof holding the aluminum foil, and the other one to tell him which direction to turn." He kissed her again, then hugged her so tightly she squeaked. "We just found Podly," he whispered.

"Let's not start celebrating just yet," she warned. "For all we know, Roger AuClair dismantled the data bank and is using it for a tea tin."

Luke dragged her to the snowcat. "Don't even think it!"

Camry sat at the rickety old table in the ramshackle old cabin, sipping the peppermint tea Roger had made her before he'd taken Max and Tigger outside to supervise Luke as he repaired the dish.

The cabin sported two rooms, the dividing wall fashioned from mismatched snowshoes;

several broken skis; and a large number of crooked sticks—some with the bark carefully removed to expose beautiful knots. An assortment of dishes and dented pots were neatly stacked on shelves beneath a sagging counter holding a pockmarked enamel sink and hand pump that looked more rusty than solid. The large wood cookstove sitting in the center of the sidewall, radiating the heat of a sauna, was covered with cast-iron pots wafting up steam that smelled of citrus and cloves.

Basically, Cam might have thought she was sitting smack in the middle of the nineteenth century but for the giant flat-screened television hanging on the opposite wall. On each side of it, rising from floor to rafter, were shelves crammed full of books. Sitting just a few feet in front of the television was a fine-grained leather recliner that looked as if it belonged in a New York penthouse. And tucked into every available nook and cranny scattered around the cabin were what appeared to be pieces of Podly—some the size of a gum stick, some as big as a basketball.

She did not, however, see anything that resembled a data bank.

Hearing Luke's footsteps on the roof—which creaked threateningly under his weight—Cam reached into her coat and pulled Podly's transmitter out of the pocket. She stood up to glance out the window and saw Roger sitting on the ground, fighting back two ecstatic dogs as he called instructions up to Luke.

Cam looked down at the transmitter. "I don't know what you're up to, Fiona," she whispered as she started walking around the cabin, holding the tiny instrument out in front of her. "But if this is about that bib I gave you that said *Shamans Rock,* you're a smart enough girl to know that I was only trying to piss off your daddy. You're going to grow up to be a wonderful drùidh just like your parents, probably even more powerful. And really, I truly enjoyed spending time with you this past week—even if you were only messing with me. But please, Fiona, don't mess with Luke. He's such a good man, and he's trying so hard to make up for eavesdropping on Podly. Help me help him find the data bank . . . in one piece," she tacked on as she continued around the cabin.

"A-and while you're at it, could you help me figure out if this ache in my chest is because I love Luke more than I fear the magic? Because if that's what's making my heart hurt, then I'm afraid you're also going to have to help me find the courage to do something about it."

The little transmitter suddenly chirped, and Cam stilled on an indrawn breath. "Where?" she whispered, moving the instrument left and then right.

It chirped again when she started walking toward the front of the cabin, giving a series of beeps that increased in frequency. As she waved it back and forth like a homing device, it eventually led her to the front wall, then started vibrating when she passed it near a dusty old frame hanging at eye level.

It took Cam a moment to realize she was looking at some sort of certificate. She pulled down the sleeve of her sweater, rubbed away the dust, and suddenly frowned.

Roger AuClair was a justice of the peace?

She squinted to read the date, but the ink was smudged by what appeared to be a thumbprint. June something, the year two thousand and . . . something.

She held the transmitter next to the frame, and it started vibrating excitedly again. Cam's heart thumped madly, and a flurry of butterflies took flight in her belly. "What are you saying?" she whispered.

The cabin door beside her suddenly opened, startling Cam into tossing the transmitter into the air with a gasp of surprise. It bounced off an equally startled Roger, causing Luke to bump into him when the old hermit stopped in midstep. All three of them watched as the transmitter clattered to the floor, rolled up against the leather recliner, and loudly chirped.

Roger walked over and picked it up just as Max tried to grab it. "Dag-nab-it, what are you doing back here, you infernal thing?" he asked the instrument. He held it toward Camry. "You make it stop that blasted noise, Missy MacKeage, or I swear I'm going to take my shotgun to it."

When Cam only gaped at him, he thrust the transmitter toward Luke. "I thought I'd seen the last of this blasted thing when I gave it to Fiona."

Luke stopped in midreach. "Did you say *Fiona*? She was here?"

"Of course she was here." Roger slapped the transmitter into Luke's hand. "Who do you think told me to expect you?"

"Fiona *Gregor*?" Luke glanced uncertainly at Camry. "How old is she?"

Roger's eyebrows drew together. "Yes, Gregor. And I never know how old she's going to be when she shows up." He held his arm out at eye level. "But this time she was in her teens, about yea-high, with long blond hair and big blue eyes." He kissed his fingers with a loud smack. "And she bakes the sweetest pies this side of heaven."

"When was Fiona here?" Camry asked.

"Well, let me see," Roger murmured, smoothing

down his shaggy white beard, then tapping his fingers against it as if counting. "Last time, it was almost three weeks ago." He nodded toward the transmitter. "I bartered her six apple pies for that thing. But what she didn't know was that I would have given it to her for free." He suddenly scowled, pointing at them. "But don't you go telling her that when you see her, you hear? It would hurt her feelings," he said with a nod. "She was beside herself happy, thinking she was getting the best end of the bargain, 'cause I didn't tell her it suddenly starts squawking for no reason. I spent the good part of last summer tearing this cabin apart looking for a mouse before I realized it was *that* thing making those little noises."

Camry inched closer to Luke and slipped her hand into his, taking a fortifying breath when he quietly squeezed it. "I noticed you're a justice of the peace, Mr. AuClair, and I was wondering if you perform weddings?" she asked, squeezing Luke's hand in return when he stiffened. "And what you might charge for your services."

"Well now," Roger said, his eyes glinting in the setting sunlight coming through the open door. "That would depend on what you might have that I'd want." He arched one bushy brow. "I'd be willing to barter for that big dog of yours, seeing as how I lost my own faithful black friend almost thirteen years ago. He wasn't half as handsome as your Max, what with his missing part of one ear and his eyes being foggy, but he was all heart, I tell you." He nodded. "I'd marry you two up for Max, but you can keep Tigger. She's friendly enough, but she don't seem all that practical, what with having almost no legs and needing to wear that prissy sweater."

"I'm sorry, but Max is—"

"Will you please excuse us, Mr. AuClair?" Luke said, cutting Cam off by dragging her out the door. "We'll just be a moment."

Luke led her a fair distance from the cabin, then spun around to face her. "Mind telling me what you're up to?" he asked, a distinct edge in his voice.

"I'm accepting your proposal."

"Now? You want some crazy old hermit to marry us?" He took hold of her shoulders. "Camry, this isn't the time or the place. I asked you to marry me only hours ago, and that's not enough time for you to make that kind of decision."

Cam's heart started pounding so hard that her ribs actually hurt. "A-are you having second thoughts?"

"No!" His hands on her shoulders tightened. "But if we're not legally married, then you won't believe you're trumping the universe."

"But he's a real justice of the peace. I saw his certificate hanging on the wall."

"That certificate is probably as old as the cabin."

"No, it was issued to Roger AuClair by the state of Maine in the year two thousand and something. It's real. It even has the Maine seal on it."

"But we don't have a license. Or witnesses. And I'm not an American citizen. This isn't a decision you can make in a few hours and then do in two minutes."

"You young folks needn't worry about the paperwork," Roger said, waving some papers as he walked toward them. "You'll be legally wed. Fiona brought me your license," Roger continued when Luke spun around in surprise. He handed the papers to him. "She filled out all your information, and she even signed as your witness."

"That's impossible." Luke scanned the page, then flipped over to the next page. "Who in hell is this other witness, Thomas Gregor Smythe?" he asked, turning to Cam when she gasped.

"H-he's an old hermit who used to live in Pine Creek. And he's also Winter's . . . grandson," she whispered, her heartache turning to dread when Luke took a step back.

She glanced briefly at Roger AuClair, then back at Luke. Only instead of calmly explaining what she finally realized was going on, Cam suddenly threw herself into his arms. "I've spent my whole life running from the magic!" she cried. "And instead of hating me for it, the magic gave me you!" She looked up, blinking back tears as she clutched his jacket. "Please, Luke, I need you to love me uncompromisingly, unpretentiously, and . . . and unconditionally," she ended in a desperate whisper.

Luke took hold of her shoulders and held her away from him. "But the real Fiona Gregor is only five months old. And her mother is younger than you are. Thomas Smythe can't be Winter's grandson, because he isn't even been born yet," he growled. "None of this is making any sense, Camry."

"Miracles don't have to make sense," Roger interjected, drawing Luke's attention. "That's the *unconditional* part of love, Renoir. It's what causes a mangy old pound mutt to hold on to a child who would love him forever for nearly an hour, and compels a mother to wait twenty years," he said, looking at Cam, "letting the secret to ion propulsion orbit the world until her daughter is ready to take ownership of her destiny." He nodded toward the papers Luke held crushed in his fist. "And it's opportunities given to those courageous enough to look deep inside themselves, and accept what they see—flaws and all—as the miracles they are.

"It's not the magic you've been running from, Camry," he continued gently. "It's your extraordinary passion for life. Your baby sister's powers have always seemed so overwhelming that you assumed you had none of your own. But the magic works for everyone, including those who won't accept it, and those who don't understand it." He shot her a wink, gesturing toward Luke. "*Especially* those who don't understand it."

"Wh-who are you, really?" she whispered.

He smoothed down the front of his tattered coat with a shrug. "Let's just say I'm a very old distant relative, shall we?" He puffed out his chest. "But I assure you both, I have the authority—and the means—to make your marriage legal and binding. That is, if you're both brave enough to follow your hearts."

He held up his hand when she tried to ask him another question. "As for your little worry about getting pregnant, let me assure you that the choice has *always* been yours. And now Luke's, too, of course," he added with a nod. "Your sisters knew they wanted children, so Providence simply granted each of them their wish—though maybe not quite *when* they wished," he added with a chuckle.

He held his arms out to encompass their surroundings. "To put this in terms you folks *can* understand, life is really nothing more than an infinite, interconnected matrix. It runs on a rather simple equation for the most part, only appearing complex when you factor in *free will*. And free will always trumps Providence," he said, giving Camry another wink. "So just take having a child out of the equation, both of you, as you look deep inside yourselves and acknowledge the miracle Fiona has asked you to be for each other."

He dropped his hands to his sides with a shrug. "You can't make a mistake if you follow your heart. Not if you have the courage to go where it leads you. There are no wrong decisions, only the consequence of not making any decision at all by running away from life instead of toward it," he ended gently, his eyes warm and his smile encouraging.

Absolute silence settled around them.

Roger AuClair suddenly rubbed his hands together, his expression turning expectant. "So, people, are we having a wedding or not? 'Cause if'n I can't have the dog, then it's gonna cost you that fancy snow machine you drove up in, and that's my final offer," he declared, his old hermit persona suddenly returning.

He frowned when Cam and Luke continued standing silently, staring at him.

"Okay then," he said, holding his hands up,

palms toward them. "I can see you need to think on it some. I'll leave you to discuss it between you then, 'cause I know you two people are intelligent enough not to take marriage lightly—seeing as how you each hold a handful of fancy school degrees." He spun around and headed to the cabin, Max and Tigger bounding after him. "Just don't take too long, 'cause if you're not hitched before *Survivorman* comes on, you'll be unzipping those sleeping bags and finding yourselves camped at opposite ends of my cabin." He stopped at the door and looked back at them, his sharp green eyes gleaming with amusement. " 'Cause until I give my blessing, the *entire* amusement park is shut down."

Chapter Fifteen

"When did you tell him about Maxine?" Luke quietly asked when Roger disappeared inside the cabin.

"I didn't."

"Then how did he know what happened to Kate thirteen years ago?" He held the papers toward her. "And this license; how could Fiona have given it to him three weeks ago, before she even met me? Every bit of information on here is correct, right down to my biological father's name."

Camry said nothing, staring at the papers in his hand.

Luke lifted her chin to make her look at him. "How can Roger AuClair possibly know so much about us?" he asked, fighting the alarm tightening his gut. "Even your amusement park comment. It's almost as if he's been listening to our conversations for the past week."

Luke suddenly drove his hand into his pocket and pulled out the transmitter. "This," he growled, holding it up between them. "It's not a transmitter, it's some sort of listening device!" He wound his arm back and threw it, watching it shatter into pieces against a tree, then took hold of Camry's hand and started toward the snowcat. "I can't explain what's going on, much less why, but we are getting the hell off this mountain."

He opened the door and tried to lift her inside, but Camry pulled free and took several steps back.

"Oh, right. The dogs." He headed toward the cabin.

"No, Luke!" she cried, grabbing his arm and spinning around. "Wait. I can explain," she said, her eyes searching his. "I-it's the magic," she whispered. "I know you don't believe in anything but cold hard facts," she rushed on, clutching his arms to follow him when he took a step back. "But the very energy that powers *you and me* is the exact same energy that powers the universe. From the cradle, I've been taught that it's *the magic* that powers life—quietly, benevolently, and . . . and unpretentious in its desire to see each of us reach our full potential."

She dropped her gaze to his chest. "And I've spent my entire adult life running from it." She looked up, smiling sadly. "Until I woke up one morning to find a handsome, sexy, unassuming rocket scientist in my bed, who didn't seem to take me anywhere near as seriously as I took myself."

"I've always taken you seriously," Luke barely managed to say.

She let go of him and hugged herself, her smile turning self-abasing as she shook her head in denial. "I've been so full of myself, it's a wonder my head fits through doors. I've blamed all my problems on everyone but myself; my mother wouldn't collaborate with me, some jerk in France was trying to steal my work, all my sisters were so damned happy I wanted to kick them, and . . ." She reached up and clasped his face in her shaking hands. "And then *you* magically appeared. And for the first time in a very long time, I wanted to be damned happy, too. With you."

She wrapped her arms around his waist and pressed her cheek to his pounding heart. "Over this past week, I found myself falling in love with a man who sees brick walls as opportunities, a belligerent colleague as a challenge, and a grumpy roommate as an intimate partner."

She tilted her head back to look up at him, and Luke's knees turned to jelly at the raw, unadulterated truth he saw in her tear-filled eyes.

"I want to spend forever with you, Luke, seeing life the way you see it. I didn't need a few hours to consider your proposal; I only needed the courage to admit to myself that I love you so much, my heart hurts when I think about a future that doesn't include you. I've never felt this alive, Luke. Normally that would scare the hell out of me, but *you* make me brave."

She covered his mouth with her fingers when he tried to speak. "There's more," she whispered. "A-and it's important that you hear it from me." She stepped out of his arms—making Luke's knees nearly buckle—and squared her shoulders on a shuddering breath. "Roger AuClair's eyes look familiar to you because they're the mirror image of my father's eyes, and mine, and those of every other MacKeage born since the beginning of time. Only Winter has blue eyes, like my mother. And Fiona." She gestured toward the cabin. "If I had to guess, I would say Roger is one of my original ancestors, born in a time when the magic was honored instead of held suspect like it is today. Which is why he's appeared to you—to *us*—as a harmless old hermit."

She held her arms out from her sides. "I am

of the highland clan MacKeage, and loving me means accepting the magic that rules our science." She swiped away a tear running down her cheek, her beautiful green eyes locked on his, her vulnerability fully exposed. "So if you still want to spend the rest of your life with me after all you've seen today, and can wrap your mind around the notion that it's only the tip of the iceberg, then I would ask that you let Roger marry us—right now, in this magical place."

Luke's legs finally buckled and he dropped to his knees, holding his arms out to her. Camry threw herself at him with a cry of relief, and hugged him so tight he grunted.

"Right now, right here," he said into her hair. He tilted her head back. "But only because I happen to be insanely in love with you," he growled, covering her mouth with his.

"Okay, then!" Roger AuClair called out as he walked to them. "Let's get these vows said before you folks set these poor dogs to blushing!"

Luke forced himself to stop making delicious love to Camry's mouth and looked up, only to blink at the man dressed in . . . wearing a . . .

Camry covered his gaping mouth with her hand. "Don't ask, Luke, just accept," she said, leaning her forehead against his with a giggle. "It's a drùidh thing."

"It'll be a first for me," Roger said, "but if you two want to give your vows on your knees, I don't mind none."

Luke scrambled to his feet, pulling Camry with him and immediately tucking her up against his side as he faced what he could only describe as . . . honest to God, the man looked like a fairy-tale *wizard*. Roger AuClair was wearing a black-and-gold spun robe that billowed to the ground, a thick leather belt encrusted with enough jewels to ransom a nation, and a pointed hat that looked an awful lot like the one Mickey Mouse wore in the Disney movie *Fantasia*—which Luke must have watched a hundred times with Kate.

"Would you folks be wanting the *short* version, or the really, really long one that will probably run over into my *Survivorman* show?" Roger asked. He suddenly shot Luke a broad smile. "I see your fancy degrees *are* worth the paper they're printed on, Renoir. I'm getting all my channels now."

"Thank you," Luke said. "And we'd like the short version, please."

The old hermit started patting himself down, until his hand suddenly disappeared inside his robe, only to reappear holding a book that had to weigh fifteen pounds if it weighed an ounce. He started leafing through the pages, murmuring to himself.

Luke glanced down at Camry tucked under his

arm, and found her smiling up at him. She patted his chest. "Don't worry, the amusement park will be open all night."

"I might be old, missy, but I'm not deaf," Roger muttered, still leafing through his tome. "Okay then," he said, his voice booming with authority as he launched into a guttural litany that sounded more spat than spoken.

"Excuse me," Luke interrupted. "That's not Latin."

Roger shot him a dark look. "It's Gaelic." He looked back down at his book with a heavy sigh. "Now I have to start all over."

Which he did.

"But how am I supposed to know what I'm vowing?" Luke asked.

Roger stopped in midsputter with a fuming glare aimed at Camry. "Shut him up, missy, or you're going to find yourself married to a toad."

Camry bumped Luke's hip. "Quit interrupting him."

Luke leaned down to whisper in her ear. "Can he really turn me into a toad?"

Roger sighed heavily again. "You have the whole rest of your lives for her to explain the magic, Renoir. Can we *please* get this done?" He looked up at the sky, then back at Luke. "My show starts in twenty minutes."

Luke suddenly realized the sun had set, and it was completely dark out. Except that the three of them seemed to be standing in some sort of glowing light, which appeared to be emanating from Roger. Luke wiped a trembling hand over his face.

The magic that rules our science, Camry had called it.

Whereas he was thinking *insanity* might be more accurate.

Roger launched into his litany again for what sounded like a sum total of eight or ten sentences, then suddenly stopped and looked at Camry expectantly.

"I do," she said.

Roger turned his expectant look on Luke.

Oh, what the hell. "I do," he firmly echoed.

Roger closed his book with a snap. "You may exchange your rings now," he said with a regal nod.

Luke felt Camry's shoulders slump. "We don't have rings," she said.

"We didn't exactly plan to get married today," Luke drawled, giving Camry a bolstering squeeze. "We'll go straight to a jeweler when we get to Pine Creek."

"You should wear the rings Fiona gave you," Roger said. "They're her wedding present to you. She went to a lot of trouble to find just the right stone to make them."

"Fiona never gave us any rings," Camry said.

Roger's eyebrows lifted into the rim of his pointed hat. "She didn't? But she said she intended to present them in a container that had very special meaning to both of you. She even showed me the paper she was going to wrap it up in. It was deep blue, covered with glittering gold stars."

Luke stiffened.

"The transmitter!" Camry said with a gasp. She bolted out of Luke's embrace and ran toward the tree where he'd thrown it.

"Come on, AuClair," Luke said, falling in behind the dogs bounding after her. "We need your light."

Luke immediately got down on his knees beside Camry and started searching the snow. "Don't worry, we'll find them," he assured her, picking up and discarding tiny pieces of metal debris.

"Here! I found one!" Camry cried, holding something up. She suddenly tossed it away. "No, it's just a rubber O-ring."

Luke shoved Max out of the way, then snatched something out of Tigger's mouth. He held it up to the light Roger was emanating. "This could be one of them." He handed it to Camry. "It seems to be made out of some sort of stone."

She also held it up to Roger's light, then looked

at Luke. "It's black-and-white-speckled rock, just like the stone Kate gave you. Where's your pebble, Luke?"

"In my pocket," he said, reaching into his pants pocket. Only when he didn't find it, he reached into his other pocket. When he still didn't find it, he stood up and started shoving his hands into every pocket he had. He suddenly stilled, looking down at her. "I lost it."

"No, *this* is the special rock Kate gave you," she said, holding it up to him.

Luke took the smooth stone circle from her, which certainly appeared to have been cut from the tiny rock Kate had given him. "But that's impossible. I distinctly remember it was in my pocket this morning."

Roger snorted, looking at Camry. "You sure you want to marry a man who doesn't believe in anything but cold hard facts? The deed's not fully done, missy; I haven't given my blessing yet. You can still back out."

Camry dropped down onto all fours and started searching the snow again. "I'm not backing out," she muttered. "Luke, help me find your ring. That one must be mine, because it's too small for your finger."

By God, he wasn't backing out, either! He didn't care if he *was* losing his mind, as long as he lost it with Camry. Luke got down beside her and resumed searching.

"What I can't figure out," Roger said, peering over their shoulders—his light actually helping them—"is how Fiona's thoughtful gift ended up over here in the first place, all smashed to pieces."

Luke straightened to his knees, lifting a brow. "Don't you have some sort of crystal ball you can look into that will tell you?"

Roger shot him a threatening scowl. "From what I hear, women aren't all that fond of kissing toads."

Camry grabbed Luke's sleeve and tugged him back down. "Leave him alone and help me find your ring."

The light suddenly started to fade, and Luke realized that Roger was heading down the mountain. "Where are you going?" he called out.

"To unzip your sleeping bags," the old hermit muttered. "'Cause in ten minutes, I intend to be sitting in my chair, watching an all-night *Survivorman* marathon."

"I found it!" Camry cried, scrambling to her feet. She grabbed Luke's hand and ran to Roger. "Okay, we've said 'I do,' so now what?"

"Well, now you slide the rings on each other's fingers, and pledge your troths in your own words."

"But we didn't have time to write our own

vows. Wait!" she yelped when Roger turned away again. She took hold of Luke's hands and looked directly into his eyes. "I promise to love you forever, Lucian Pascal Renoir," she whispered, slipping the smooth stone ring onto his finger, "uncompromisingly, unpretentiously, and unconditionally." She shot him a crooked smile. "And I promise never to lie to you, or send you any more unladylike e-mails, or imagine ten different ways to make you beg for mercy, or—"

Luke covered her mouth with a laugh. "Let's at least keep our *vows* in the realm of reality." He lifted her hand and slid the smooth stone ring onto her finger. "And I promise you, Camry MacKeage, to love and honor you with every breath I take, forever. And I promise never to steal your work," he added with his own crooked smile. "Or lecture you until your ears fall off. And if you decide to go on any more crime sprees, I will definitely have your back."

Roger snorted. "Okay then. I guess you two do deserve each other—seeing as how you won't find anyone else willing to put up with either of you." He held his hands up, encompassing them both. "So I give my blessing to this union and pronounce you husband and wife—may God have mercy on *all* our souls," he finished with a mutter, heading toward his cabin.

"Wait. Don't I get to kiss my bride now?" Luke asked.

Roger turned and shot him a scowl. "Not until you get back to your tent." He spun back around and headed to the cabin again, patting his leg to call the dogs to him. He opened the door to let them inside, then turned back. "I'll be keeping Max and Tigger with me tonight, so the poor beasts aren't scarred for life." He pointed at the snowcat. "And you'll be walking to your tent. That fancy snow machine is now mine."

"But you can't actually *keep* it," Camry said. "We really only borrowed it from my father. We have to bring it back."

"Oh no, you don't. A deal's a deal, Missy MacKeage." He suddenly gave Luke an apologetic nod. "Excuse me, I meant *Missus Renoir*. Which means she's your problem now." He looked back at Camry. "For which your papa will be so grateful, I'm sure he would want me to have the machine for my role in getting you off his hands."

When Camry started toward the old man, Luke spun her around and started down the mountain. "Come on, *Missus* Renoir," he said with a laugh. "Before he turns *you* into a toad."

Chapter Sixteen

With the rising, nearly full moon lighting their way and the crunch of the cold snow keeping rhythm with their breathing, their mile walk to the tent was made in silence. Cam assumed Luke was trying to assimilate all that had happened. And though she would have loved to explain Roger to him, and Fiona, and the seemingly unrelated chain of events that had brought them to be walking hand in hand tonight toward the rest of their lives together, she honestly didn't know how to explain something she barely comprehended herself. The only thing she did know for sure was that she loved Luke more than she loved anything else in the world—even her beloved science.

She suddenly stopped walking.

"What is it?" Luke asked, stepping around to take hold of her shoulders. "Are you getting cold feet?" He chuckled softly. "Figuratively speaking, I mean?"

She looked up at him in wonder. "No. I suddenly just realized that the only thing more powerful than my mother's love for her work is her love for Daddy. Because if I had to choose between you and my work, I'd choose you."

"Ahh, sweetheart," Luke said, hugging her to him, then squeezing her tightly. "Grace never had to choose between anything, because she knew she could have it all." He leaned back to smile down at her. "I only spent a few days with your parents, but it was long enough for me to see that your father doesn't have to be a scientist to understand your mother's passion for her work. He appears to be her biggest fan, supporting her a hundred and ten percent. Didn't he build her that beautiful lab?"

"Yes."

"He didn't steal anything from your mother, Camry, he *empowered* her. And I bet he also encouraged all you girls to go after your own dreams, didn't he?"

"Sometimes to the point that we wanted to scream."

"And hasn't your mother always supported your *father's* passion? TarStone Mountain Ski Resort couldn't have become a world-class destination on its own."

She smiled up at him. "I guess that's another thing we can add to our definition of love: its ability to expand exponentially. It's not at all constraining, it's *unlimiting*."

He kissed the tip of her nose with a delighted laugh. "And are you ready to add one more passion to your expanding list, Mrs. Renoir? Say . . . something that involves our getting naked together?"

She toyed with the zipper on his jacket. "I-I've heard that when a person gets on a Ferris wheel the first time, the ride can be somewhat scary."

He kissed the top of her head, then took her hand and led her toward the tent. "Naw, it's only scary for the faint of heart. With your highlander genes, it's more likely the person you're riding with who'll be scared."

Cam stopped just as she was about to unzip the tent flap and looked up.

Luke was scared?

Well, damn. She'd been so focused on her own worry about finally going all the way, she hadn't even thought about what he must be feeling. Hell, what man wanted the responsibility of introducing a thirty-two-year-old virgin to lovemaking?

She unzipped the tent and crawled inside, then poked her head out to stop him from following. "Can you give me a few minutes?" she asked. "I'll start the heater and warm up the tent."

"Oh, sure. I'm sorry. Of course," he said, jumping up and quickly stepping away. He shoved his hands in his pockets. "You take as long as you need."

Luke stood in the middle of the tote road, staring up at the night sky, and fingered the perfectly sized stone ring on his left hand as he thought about all that had happened this afternoon.

Or had it really started long before today? Could finding himself on this mountain, married to the woman of his dreams, have actually begun over a year ago, when he'd tapped the key on his computer that had put him in contact with Podly? At the time, he had assumed the sheer magnitude of what he'd just done was what had caused that spark to run up his arm, jolting him to his very core. Only now he wasn't so sure it had been guilt making his heart pound wildly, but rather the distinct feeling that some tiny, unseen hand had *pushed* his hovering finger down on that button.

Was it truly possible that an imp of a girl, with piercing blue eyes and a contagious smile, could already have been working her magic?

Luke looked over at the tent glowing in the cold dark night, the lantern inside casting the movements of a faint but decidedly feminine silhouette. After today, he had to believe that anything was possible, the undeniable proof being that he had just married the most remarkable, most outrageous, sexiest woman he'd ever met.

The true miracle here, as far as he was concerned, was that Camry loved *him*.

"You must be freezing, Luke. Come in here and let me warm you up."

"I'll be right along," he called back.

Luke sucked in a deep breath of cold air, hoping to free the knot that had started forming in his gut during their walk down the mountain. For as focused as he'd been these last few days on actually getting to use one of his condoms . . . well, everything had changed in the maintenance garage, when he had realized that he wasn't just in lust with Camry: he was in love with her.

But even in his wildest dreams, he hadn't expected his honeymoon suite to be a tent, his wedding bed a sleeping bag, or his marriage to be blessed by a . . . wizard.

And he sure as hell hadn't expected his bride to be a virgin.

"Vroom! Vroom!"

Luke snapped his gaze to the tent.

"Oh my God, Luke, did you hear that? The Ferris wheel is starting without you! Get in here before you miss the ride!"

Luke dropped his chin to his chest, the knot in his gut unraveling on a strangled laugh. What was he doing standing out here worrying about his lovemaking living up to Camry's expectations, when he should be worried about surviving *hers*?

He unzipped his jacket and ran to the tent. "You keep your hands away from those controls, lady!" he barked out, dropping to his knees in front of the tent. "It takes an experienced operator who knows what he's doing to start up that Ferris wheel." He pulled his sweater and long-john top over his head, then unbuckled his belt and shoved down his pants. "If you push the wrong button, it could take me all night to get it running correctly."

"Vroom, vroom," she purred with a giggle. "Oh! I think I found it, Luke. Quick, get in here and tell me if this is the right button."

He had to sit on his jacket to unlace his boots, but instead of undoing them, he ended up with a handful of knots. "Stop playing with the equipment!" He tugged on the mess he'd made of his laces, which only served to tighten them. "That's my job!"

When her purr turned to a lusty moan, Luke

pulled his multitool out of its pouch and cut the laces on both boots. He shoved off his pants and long-john bottoms, then turned and crawled into the tent. "Do you have any idea what the penalty is for messing with such delicate equip—" Luke snapped his mouth shut on an indrawn breath. "My God, you're beautiful," he whispered.

"You're not so bad yourself," she whispered back, opening her arms to him.

But instead of covering her body with his, he settled beside her, propped his head on his hand, and let his gaze travel over her beautiful, naked, inviting body. "Exactly which button did you push that made that wonderful noise?" he asked.

"The 'vroom, vroom'?"

"No, that sweet little lusty moan."

"Oh, that noise." She pointed down at her belly. "You could try pressing here and see what happens."

Luke dipped his finger into her belly button, and she gasped loudly.

"Nope, that's not it," he muttered, walking his fingers toward her breasts.

She immediately stopped him. "Your hands are cold."

Luke flopped onto his back and folded his cold hands behind his head. "Then I guess the amusement park's shut down until they warm up."

"Maybe I can hurry the process along," she murmured, rolling over and crawling on top of him. She walked her warm fingers up his chest to his shoulders, and leaned down and touched her lips to his. "I wonder what buttons you have," she said into his mouth. "And what sort of noises I can get *you* to make."

She certainly got a groan out of him when she wiggled her hips up the length of his shaft just as her mouth took possession of his. And while she made delicious love to his mouth, Luke tried to think where he'd put his ditty bag.

He suddenly bolted upright, wrapping his arms around her to keep her from falling. "Dammit, the condoms are in the snowcat!"

She leaned away to see his eyes. "We don't really need them . . . do we?"

"That is one decision we are not making today."

She shot him a smug smile. "Then we'll just have to use the condoms I brought."

Luke reared back. "*You* brought condoms?"

"Don't brilliant minds think alike? You're not the only horny toad in this tent."

Luke shuddered. "Let's not refer to ourselves as toads, okay?"

"Ohhhh, do that again," she said on a moan, wiggling intimately against him. "I think you just found one of my buttons."

Luke held himself perfectly still. "The condoms."

"Under my pillow," she murmured, pulling his face toward hers so she could attack his mouth again.

Luke blindly felt behind him for her pillow while she conveniently worked herself into a really good frenzy, kissing him senseless and running her hands over his shoulders, her nails sending shivers coursing through him. But he suddenly stilled again when he found the condoms and counted out three sleeves.

Three packs per sleeve equaled nine.

Holy hell, did she think he was Superman?

He snatched up one of the sleeves, wrestled his mouth from hers, and set her away. She immediately snatched the packs out of his hand, tore one open, then scooted down his legs and started to roll the condom down over him.

Luke gritted his teeth against the explosion of sensation—both visual and tactile—that shot through every cell in his body as she awkwardly attempted to sheath him. The lantern cast its glow on her beautiful breasts, her movements making her peaked nipples brush his thighs. Her hands caressed his scrotum as her fingers slowly slid down the length of his shaft, and Luke felt beads of sweat break out on his forehead. Which was why just as soon as she was done, he snatched her hands away and rolled on top of her.

"My turn to drive you insane," he growled, settling between her thighs.

She immediately lifted her hips, her hands clutching his shoulders. "Yes, make me insane," she pleaded with ragged urgency. "I want to feel you inside me, Luke. Deep, where I ache."

Her tension was palpable, her desire desperate. Searching for any sign of discomfort, Luke eased himself down until he was poised to enter her, then reached between them and caressed her intimately. She was surprisingly moist and slick and ready for him—except that she seemed to be holding her breath.

"If you pass out, you're going to miss the best part," he said with a forced laugh, feeling somewhat desperate himself. He kissed the tip of her nose, then locked his gaze back onto hers. "Close your eyes and picture yourself opening up for me. Feel me sliding into you this first time, Camry, and savor each little rippling sensation."

He lowered more of his weight and pressed into her, feeling her stretch to accommodate him as he brushed his lips over her eyelids, then trailed tiny kisses across her cheek. "Lift your hips," he said into her ear. "And meet me halfway."

He felt her heels press into the sleeping bag

beside his thighs, and Luke slipped deeper as she lifted toward him. "Feel yourself surrounding me, making me yours," he continued soothingly when her breath caught on a gasp.

He seated himself fully, capturing her sound of distress in his mouth, then immediately stilled, lifting his head to smile into her wondrous eyes. "Hello, wife."

She hesitantly smiled back. "H-hello, husband."

"Are you okay?"

She thought about that, then nodded. "I'm okay. S-so that's it? This is what I've been missing all these years?"

Luke arched a brow. "What exactly were you expecting?"

"Well," she said, the corners of her mouth turning up, "I guess I expected fireworks or something. Or at the very least, some moaning and shouting."

He raised his other brow. "I heard moaning."

Two flags of red appeared in her cheeks. "I meant from you."

"Oh. Well, Mrs. Renoir, just as soon as you give me the nod that it's okay to move, I'll see if I can't scare up some moaning and shouting."

"So that's what's wrong with this Ferris wheel? It's not *moving*?" She made a tsking sound. "And you said you were an experienced operator. Um . . . why are you trembling?" she asked, her hands flexing on his shoulders.

"Because you are so damn hot and tight and beautiful, it's taking every ounce of strength I possess not to drive into you like a mindless idiot."

Her eyes widened, her mouth forming a perfect O.

Feeling his restraint slipping, Luke forced a smile. "Here's an idea: Why don't you move first?"

The second she tentatively squirmed—which sent rockets of pleasure shooting through him—Luke realized that had been a really bad idea. He dropped his forehead to hers with a groan. "No, don't move."

"I'm sorry. Am I *too* damn hot and tight and beautiful for you?"

He snapped his head up to stare down at her, and found her smiling at him.

"Vroom-vroom, husband," she whispered.

The last thread of his restraint broke on a bark of laughter. Luke dropped to his elbows to lace his fingers through her hair, and attacked her mouth as he lifted his hips just enough to push into her again. Swallowing her moan of pleasure, he repeated the action, rising back up so he could watch the play of emotions on her face.

Her hands moved from his shoulders to his

chest, her fingers kneading into him, her encouraging mewls growing demanding. Her breathing turned ragged as he increased his rhythm, and Luke felt her tightening with building energy as she rose up to meet his thrusts. He reached between them and caressed her, watching her eyes glass over as she arched up into his touch.

"Come with me, Luke!" she cried, her breathing growing more ragged as she moved restlessly, straining toward her release.

Luke rose to his knees, grasped her hips, and pulled her into his thrusts. He wanted to whisper encouragement but found he was beyond speech, every fiber of his being completely focused on the explosion building inside her.

He suddenly stilled, holding her high on his thighs, and reached down and caressed her again. Her climax broke with a cry of utter abandon, and she tightened around him in pulsing waves of molten heat.

His own climax hit hard and fast, tearing a shout from his throat as her wild convulsions pulled him into the maelstrom, his mind emptying of all thoughts save one: that *miracles* packed one hell of a powerful wallop.

Chapter Seventeen

"I am *so* going to kill my sisters," Cam muttered as soon as she could speak, her racing heart
threatening to crack her ribs.

"Why?"

"For neglecting to mention how mind-blowing
sex really is."

Luke rolled toward her and propped his head
on his hand. "Mind-blowing, huh?"

Silently thanking her very wise mother for
teaching all her daughters about the delicate
subtleties of the male ego, Cam reached over and
patted Luke's heaving chest. "I'm sure it was because I had such an experienced operator at the
controls."

He grunted agreement, then flopped onto his back. "So long as you realize that it wouldn't have been mind-blowing with any of your old boyfriends. If they were so dumb they didn't even realize they weren't having sex, they sure as hell wouldn't have known which buttons to push, much less *when*."

Cam snuggled against him with a sigh of utter contentment, her amused smile turning into a yawn. "You better get some sleep," she murmured, resting her cheek on his thumping heart. "Because just as soon as I get my strength back, I'm going to start pushing *your* buttons."

Luke was reluctant to open his eyes, worried that if Camry knew he was awake she might attack him again. The insatiable woman had somehow managed to keep the Ferris wheel running all night, at times so fast that he'd gotten dizzy. She'd also managed to put a healthy dent in her stash of condoms, and Luke decided he was buying himself a red cape and a T-shirt with a large *S* on the front of it.

"Are you awake?" she asked from the depths of the sleeping bag, where her cold nose was pressed into his ribs.

"No."

"Is the sun up?"

"It must be, since I can see my breath."

The edge of the sleeping bag folded back, and two sleepy green eyes blinked up at him. "I suppose we're going to have to get dressed and go rescue Max and Tigger before Roger spoils them rotten."

"That sounds like a plan," Luke said, not moving. "You trudge right up there and save them while I stay here and pack up camp."

"Oh no." She threw off the sleeping bag and immediately started scrambling into her clothes. "You're coming with me."

"He's *your* long-lost relative. You should spend some quality time alone with him before we leave," he said, sitting up and looking around for his long johns. Finally remembering he'd undressed outside, he pulled the sleeping bag back up around his shoulders. "Can you reach outside and get my clothes?" he asked, seeing as how she was already mostly dressed. "The heater must have run out of fuel."

"Hours ago." She poked her head out the tent flap—giving him a really nice view of her really nice backside—then reappeared with his clothes and boots. "It looks like it's been snowing quite a while," she said, shaking the snow off his long johns before handing them to him. "And you have to go to Roger's with me so you can help me steal the snowcat back."

"Well, why not," he said with a snort, slipping into his cold clothes. "What could possibly go wrong stealing from a man who can turn us into toads? At least we're keeping our crimes in the family."

"And while we're at it, I'll distract him so you can find the data bank," she said, handing Luke his boots. "Hey, what happened to your laces?"

He put on the boots and tied what was left of the laces. "I seem to remember something about you starting the honeymoon without me."

She blinked at him, her cheeks flushing a dull red.

Luke cupped her face in his hands. "Good morning, wife."

"We're really married, aren't we?" she whispered back.

"After last night, I certainly hope so."

"Any second thoughts?"

"Only that our honeymoon suite was a tent instead of a five-star room in Tahiti."

"Oh no! I love that our wedding night was out here in the wilderness." She pulled his hands down to hold them in hers. "The tent was cozy and intimate, and I swear it was like we were the only two people on Earth." Her eyes sparkled with humor. "And there's also the added bonus that only the animals heard you shouting for mercy."

"Okay, that does it," he growled, pushing her onto her back to pin her down with his body. "There's one more secret little button that I didn't push last night," he said, having to raise his voice over her laughter, "because I didn't want you fainting from passion overload. But now I—"

A fiberglass support suddenly snapped overhead, and the tent collapsed, billowing down around them.

"Dammit, I told you this wasn't a four-season tent." He pushed up to his hands and knees, using his body as a new tent support. "But oh no, you wanted the larger one so there would be room for the dogs. Just as soon as you stop laughing, could you maybe find the zipper and crawl out?"

He grunted when her elbow rammed his chest, then jackknifed his hips when her head butted his groin, and she fell back with a giggle. "Anytime today," he ground out, pushing at the tent to shake off some of the heavy snow. "We need to get down off the mountain before the storm intensifies."

She finally crawled outside, then held the flap open for him. Luke gave one last push at the tent, then dove for the opening just as the rest of the snow slid off the outer storm fly and down the back of his neck.

"Lovely," he said, standing up and digging the

snow out of his collar. He looked around to find that visibility was less than a quarter mile. "We've already gotten six or seven inches of heavy wet snow, but if the temperature drops and the wind kicks up, we won't be able to see past our noses."

"Roger won't really keep our snowcat, will he?" she asked, brushing more snow off his shoulders.

"If he doesn't give it back when we ask nicely, we'll just threaten to break his satellite dish so that he doesn't get *any* channels."

Camry started dismantling what was left of the tent. "I love your criminal mind."

While she rolled up the storm fly and collapsed the rest of the supports, Luke pulled everything out from inside and started making a pile of their gear to pick up on their way back. In twenty minutes they were entirely packed up, and half an hour after that, they arrived at the cabin.

Or rather, they arrived at where the cabin *should* have been.

"It's gone!" Camry cried in dismay.

"That's impossible. We must have walked right past it. The wind's picked up, making visibility worse."

"No, this is the right spot." She pointed to their right. "I distinctly remember that pine tree with the burn scar where Podly crashed. The cabin should be right here!"

"An entire building can't just suddenly vanish overnight."

She looked up at him with a gasp. "And he took Tigger and Max!"

Luke wiped a gloved hand over his face, attempting to wipe away his disbelief along with the snowflakes catching on his beard. "Okay, let's think about this. There has to be a perfectly logical explanation for why we can't find the cabin, or Roger, or the dogs." He shot her a scowl when she snorted. "An explanation *other* than magic."

"I know! A spaceship swooped down and took Roger and Tigger and Max back to Mars to add to their zoo."

Luke sighed. "That's just as plausible as anything else that's happened in the last twenty-four hours."

"Listen. Did you hear that?" She pointed to their left. "There it is again. That's Max barking. Come on!"

"Camry, wait!" Luke called out, chasing after her as she disappeared into the blinding snow. "You don't know what you might be running into!"

But when they reached the shelter of the dense evergreen trees, the visibility got considerably better. They stopped to listen again, then started running toward what sounded like both dogs barking.

They skidded to a stop when they saw Max and Tigger sitting under a huge spruce tree, in the sled made out of Podly's housing. Max immediately jumped out and ran up to them, and Tigger—wearing not only her pink sweater, but what looked like a tiny version of a wizard's hat—started yelping in protest.

"Oh, that's a good boy," Camry said, dropping to her knees to hug Max. "You helped us find you without abandoning your friend."

Luke walked over and scooped up Tigger, then reared back to avoid getting his face washed. "It's okay, Tig," he crooned. "Mommy and Daddy are here. We wouldn't have left this mountain without you."

"Mommy and Daddy?" Camry repeated with a laugh, walking up to them. She gave Tigger an affectionate scratch behind the ears, then straightened the dog's pointed little hat before looking down at the sled, which now had a small tarp fashioned like a tent over the top.

"Well, at least he made sure they were comfy. And judging by the snow on the tarp, they haven't been here more than an hour. Hey, there's something else in the sled," she said, reaching inside. She pulled out a small tin coffee can. "I don't think it's big enough to be the data bank."

Luke set Tigger back in the sled, on top of what appeared to be a straw-filled mattress, and took the tin from her—only to nearly drop it when whatever was inside suddenly chirped.

Camry snatched it from him and popped off the lid. "It's the transmitter!" she cried, pulling it out. "And it's been put back together!"

When she tried to hand it to him, Luke shoved his hands in his pockets. "That infernal thing is *possessed,*" he growled, stepping away. He suddenly groaned. "Oh, God, now I'm *talking* like Roger."

Camry stuffed the transmitter in her pocket, then reached into the can again. "There's a note," she said, pulling out an envelope. She held it toward him. "And it's addressed to you."

Luke plopped down on the ground, tucking Max up next to him. "You read it. I've had my fill of Roger AuClair and all his hocus-pocus."

She dropped down beside him, pulled a colorful card out of the envelope, and held it for him to see the front. "It's just like the ones Fiona gave us."

Luke picked up the envelope. "But this isn't Fiona's writing." He looked back at her hand. "So, what's it say?"

"*Dear Lucian,*" she read. She stopped, eyeing him with amusement.

"What?"

She looked back at the card, cleared her throat, and continued. *"You may have had enough of my hocus-pocus, young man, but I'm afraid you're going to have to put up with a bit more of it, if you're hoping to hold on to that miracle sitting beside you."*

She smiled over at him. "In case you're wondering, he's referring to me."

When Luke merely arched a brow, she looked back at the card. *"You have less than two days to get Camry back into the loving arms of her mama and papa. Actually, it's one day, nine hours, and sixteen minutes from right now. You step foot in Gù Brath even one second after the winter solstice, and your marriage to the woman of your dreams will never have happened."*

"That bastard can't do that!"

"Tsk-tsk," she said. She held the card toward him. "That wasn't me. See, he actually wrote *tsk-tsk* right here." She held the card in front of her again. *"Tsk-tsk,"* she repeated, *"it's dangerous to call a drùidh names. And though you may not believe it right now, not only am I your greatest ally, I'm also your only means of accomplishing the seemingly impossible task ahead of you. Your science will only take you so far, Dr. Renoir, before you will have to concede that there's more to life than numbers, equations, and cold hard facts."*

She stopped reading and looked at him. "What impossible task is he talking about?" she asked, her eyes filling with worry.

"He's messing with us, Camry. It won't be the first time I've walked off this mountain in a blizzard. We're both strong and healthy, and it shouldn't take us even one day to get to Pine Creek." He gestured toward the tree next to the sled. "Especially with snowshoes."

She looked where he was pointing, then back at him. "But he left only one pair."

Luke stood up and walked over to the tree, giving Tigger a pat on his way by. He looked back at Camry and smiled. "Maybe my 'seemingly impossible task' is that I'm going to have to pull you all the way home in the sled."

She didn't return his smile. "I don't like this, Luke," she whispered, her eyes darkening with concern. "Why would he say that *you* had to get me home, when I am perfectly capable of getting myself home?"

"Because the old bastard is messing with us," he repeated, walking over and sitting down beside her. He hugged her to him. "He's just a bored old hermit, Camry, who loves drama." He snorted. "He even took it so far as to dress up like a wizard for added effect."

"Then where is he?"

"Gone in our snowcat. When we get back to Pine Creek, we'll probably find it parked on Main Street. Roger will be sitting in a bar, getting folks to pay for his drinks while he tells them about the two rocket scientists he duped into believing in magic."

She leaned away. "So you didn't believe anything that happened yesterday? When you said your vows to me, you were only . . . what . . . humoring me?" She looked down at the card in her hand. "So if you believe this has all been a charade, then you also believe that we're not really married."

He placed a finger under her chin and lifted her face to look at him. "As far as I'm concerned, we became husband and wife last night. And just as soon as we get back to civilization, we're going to make it legal."

"But the magic is *real*, Luke."

He kissed the tip of her nose, then smiled. "Yes, it is, because I just spent a very magical night with a very magical woman." He gave her another kiss, this time on her mouth, then stood up. "So, Mrs. Renoir, we better get going. I'd like to at least make it down to the lake before this storm gets too intense. We can wait it out at your sister's camp lot for the night, then start out fresh in the morning."

She looked back at the card in her hand. "But there's more."

"Don't bother reading it," Luke muttered, sitting down beside the sled and putting on the snowshoes. "I'm not interested in what else Roger AuClair has to say."

Chapter Eighteen

Cam sat in the sled, rubbing her cheek against Tigger, and stared at Luke's back as he trudged through the deepening snow. She'd insisted on walking, but by the time they'd made it back to their tent site and sorted through what gear they wanted to take, she'd realized not having snowshoes of her own only slowed down their progress as the storm intensified.

She sucked in a shuddering sob, her chest hurting so much she could almost feel her heart breaking in two. Not only did Luke *not* believe in the magic, he had felt it was necessary to pretend that he did. He'd stood there as serious as a groom on his wedding day and let Roger marry them, even though he thought it was all a charade.

Or maybe *farce* was a better word.

But why? If Luke loved her like he claimed, and thought she loved him equally as much, then why couldn't he have been honest with her?

Cam buried her face in Tigger's fur, wishing for her mama. She dearly needed her mother to explain to her why she'd fallen in love with a closed-minded, patronizing . . . know-it-all. She didn't care if Lucian Pascal Renoir was handsome and sexy and smart, or even strong and brave and loyal; if he couldn't wrap his mind around the magic, then he couldn't uncompromisingly, unpretentiously, and unconditionally love her.

The sled suddenly stopped, and Luke walked back to open the side of the tarp. When she wouldn't look at him, he slid his finger under her chin and lifted her face.

He sucked in his breath. "Are you crying?" he asked, wiping his thumb over her cheek. "Goddammit, you should have told me you were cold!" He reached down and started unlacing her boots. "Is it your feet? If they hurt, that's a good sign you haven't gotten frostbite yet. I'll find us a sheltered place to build a fire."

She covered his hands to stop him. "I'm not cold."

"Then why are you crying?" She saw him suddenly stiffen. "Camry, you've got to come back to reality. What I believe about magic doesn't matter, as long as you believe that *I love you*."

"I-I told you yesterday that loving me means accepting who I am."

"I do! You're Camry MacKeage—no, dammit, Camry *Renoir*—the physicist who's been driving me nuts for over a year." He cupped her face in his palms, his thumbs gently brushing her cheeks. "The woman I fell in love with within days of meeting in person." His grip tightened. "How can I make you understand that nothing else matters but our love for each other?"

She covered his hands with her own. "By *believing*, Luke," she whispered. "By honestly believing that miracles aren't something that happen only in books and movies, and that there's really more going on than our science can explain."

He visibly recoiled, sitting back on his heels. "So are you saying you can only love a man who thinks the way you do? And that I must not really love you because I can't understand how your five-month-old niece can also be sixteen, or how an old hermit can be your long-lost ancestor as well as a drùidh?" He hesitated. "Is that what you're saying, Camry?"

Unable to face him, she looked down at Tigger. "I don't know what I'm saying," she whispered. She suddenly looked back at him. "Would you believe my mother? If Dr. Grace Sutter explained the magic to you, would you believe *her*?"

He stood up and walked to the front of the sled. "We'll discuss this later," he said, the wind carrying his words away. He settled the rope over his shoulders, then glanced back. "You make sure you tell me if you get cold."

She nodded, unable to speak past the lump in her throat. Luke called Max to his side and started off, and the sled lurched forward. Cam buried her face in Tigger's neck, the image of Luke's wounded expression burning her eyes like hot sand.

It was well after dark when they reached Megan and Jack Stone's camp lot, and Luke was more than a little surprised that they actually found it, considering they had to battle both darkness and blizzard conditions. But with the last of his reserves fading from towing Camry, Tigger, and eventually Max, as well as their minimal gear, he'd given in to Camry's plea that he let her put on the snowshoes and tow him for the last few miles. He'd finally conceded when he'd realized they were mostly downhill miles, and that they'd both be better served if he conserved his strength for tomorrow's trek.

With an efficiency of effort and a few lumber scraps they found around the lot, they used the storm fly of the tent to construct a makeshift shelter, then crawled into the sleeping bag—with the dogs—to share their body heat. Luke sandwiched Camry between himself and Max and Tigger, then fell asleep almost before he'd even closed his eyes.

But when he woke up the next morning, he was alone. He bolted upright, shouting Camry's name as he scrambled to the entrance.

"I'm right here," she called back from the shoreline. She held her arms wide. "Look, Luke. Isn't it beautiful?"

He rubbed a hand over his face, shaking off the last vestige of terror, and took a calming breath as he stood up. He blinked in the sharp sunlight breaking over the east end of the frozen lake as he looked around, surprised by how utterly calm the air felt. It was a winter wonderland as far as he could see, everything blanketed in glittering, pristine snow.

"Yes, it's beautiful," he called to her, even as he thought about how difficult that beauty was going to make today's hike. But Roger's time constraint notwithstanding, their sitting still was not an option. Luke slipped into his boots and walked to her. "How much ice do you think is on the lake?" he asked, eyeing the snow-covered expanse.

"Anywhere from six inches to a foot. But some places could be only an inch." She shook her head. "And with the snow covering everything, there's no way of telling what's safe and what isn't."

Luke bent down, scooped up some snow and rubbed it over his face, giving a shiver as the last cobwebs of sleep fell away. "Then I guess we stick to the tote road. How long have you been up?"

"Half an hour. I started a small fire and melted some snow to make soup." She gestured toward the campfire burning a few yards away. "Max and Tigger and I have already eaten. The rest is yours."

"Why didn't you wake me?" he asked, going over and lifting the pot off the coals.

"I figured you'd wake yourself up, once you got the rest you needed." She knelt down beside him, picked up a stick, and pushed the embers into a pile. "I've thought about what you said yesterday," she continued softly, not looking at him. "And I agree that we should ignore Roger's ultimatum that we get back to Gù Brath before the solstice." She glanced at him, then back down at the fire. "The only people who have any say about our being married is us. We'll get home when we get there, and we'll be legally married when we want—by *who* we want."

She took hold of his sleeve, her sharp green eyes direct, her expression defiant. "We're a team, and together we can conquer the world if we want to, and trump Providence without even breaking a sweat." She reached down, lifted his hand, and fingered his ring. "Apparently *I'm* the one who forgot that the unconditional part of love works both ways," she whispered, smiling crookedly as she raised her eyes back to his. "I love you, Luke, for *exactly* who you are."

He slowly set the pot down in the snow before he dropped it, then just as slowly pulled her into his arms and held her against him with a sigh. "Thank you," he whispered into her hair. "For loving me just that much."

She melted into him, her own sigh barely audible over the sound of slurping.

"What the . . . ?" Luke glanced down to see Tigger's nose driven into the pot of soup. "Hey, that's mine!" he yelped, grabbing the dachshund and shoving her at Camry. "Your dog was eating my soup!"

"My dog? You were the one calling himself *Daddy* yesterday."

Luke picked up the pot and sat down, holding it protectively against his chest when Max came bounding up, his tongue licking his sniffing nose. "I think we should hook *them* up to the sled and make them pull *us* today."

"Come on, guys," she said with a giggle as she

scrambled to her feet. "Let's go pack up while *Daddy* eats his breakfast. We all have a long day ahead of us. But just think about the fabulous tales you'll have to tell Suki and Ruffles when you get back," she pointed out to them, her voice trailing off as she ducked into the shelter.

Luke frowned down at his soup, then used his finger to flick a whisker off the rim before he drank right out of the pot. Hell, if he was going to play the part of a sled dog today, what was a little hair in his soup?

Chapter Nineteen

Despite the ineffectual sun hanging low in the southern sky, Luke was a ball of sweat not two hours into their trek. Breathing heavily from the incline that traveled along the ridge rising sharply to their left, he stopped in the middle of the tote road, shrugged off the rope, and flexed his shoulders. He pulled his GPS out of his pocket, punched some buttons, and realized they were only a couple of miles from the turnoff to Pine Creek, which still left another twenty-three miles after that.

"Okay, everyone walks for a while," he said, tucking the GPS back in his pocket, then putting his gloves back on. "Except Tigger, I suppose."

Camry had just set Tigger forward between her legs to stand up when a low rumbling whispered through the air. "What's that?" she asked, glancing around.

Luke looked up, adrenaline spiking through him when he saw the sheet of snow sliding down the exposed ridge above, heading straight toward them. "Avalanche!" he shouted, immediately snatching up the rope. "Stay in the sled! You won't be able to run in the deep snow!"

"Max! Come!" she cried, falling back when Luke jerked the sled and ran.

The rumble grew louder, echoing down the steep granite gorge, the snow pushing an icy wave of air ahead of it that sent chills racing up Luke's spine. He veered toward the stand of trees growing on the edge of the wash, but his snowshoes caught in the jumble of talus from previous rock-slides, and he fell to his knees. He gave one last mighty heave on the rope to pull the sled past him, Camry's scream drowned out by the wall of snow slamming into them.

The rope jerked out of his hands, then tangled on one of his snowshoes as Luke helplessly tumbled in a sea of churning white, all the while fighting not to lose contact with the sled. The noise was deafening, the snow unbelievably heavy as it meted out its endless battering. The lacing on one of his boots snapped, the snowshoe attached to it pulling the boot off his foot. His hand scraped what felt like metal, but just then the rope gave a sharp tug before ripping the other snowshoe off his boot, releasing him to continue his turbulent free fall alone.

And just as suddenly as it had begun, it ended.

Luke slammed against an unmovable object, the air rushing from his lungs in a whoosh. An eerie silence settled around him, his body sheathed in what felt like concrete, every damn cell in his body screaming in agony. The snow had packed around him like a vise, squeezing his lungs and making it nearly impossible to breathe; when he opened his eyes, he literally couldn't see past his nose.

Camry! Unable even to hear his own scream, Luke frantically wiggled back and forth to free himself. His fingers brushed what felt like bark, and as he slowly increased the cavity around him, his knee connected with the tree that had stopped his fall.

Slowly, painstakingly, he was able to work his arms up beside his head, and he dug the snow out of his ears. He stilled, listening for any sound that might tell him Camry was okay, or at least that Max had made it to safety. But when he heard only the blood pounding through his veins, Luke focused on figuring out which way was up. His guess, based on the fact that the more he wiggled the farther he settled to his left, made him start digging past his right shoulder.

His fist suddenly punched through to open air! He gritted his teeth against the protest of his battered muscles and started jackknifing his body as he pushed at the snow above him. He suddenly heard barking. "Max!" he shouted through the small opening he was creating. "That's my boy! Come on, Max!"

The opening suddenly closed when a nose drove into it, and a warm tongue shot out and touched his wrist.

"Thatta boy, Max!" Luke said with a laugh. "Come find me, boy. Dig!"

With Max digging down from the top and Luke clawing his way up, he was finally able to break his upper torso free. "Good boy!" he chortled when Max lunged at his chest and started licking his face. He pushed the dog away, pointing beside him. "Keep digging. I've got to get free so we can find Camry."

With Max's help, Luke was finally able to lever himself up and crawl on top of the snow. He immediately got to his knees and looked around. "Okay, Max. Use that wonderful nose of yours and find Camry. Come on," he said, scrambling to his feet, again ignoring his screaming muscles and the fact that he had only one boot. He clapped his hands excitedly. "Find Camry, Max!"

The Lab immediately jumped into the hole from which Luke had just emerged, and started whining and sniffing around.

"She's not in there. Come on, let's play hide-and-seek. Find Camry!" he repeated, slapping his leg to urge the dog out. "And Tigger. Let's go find Tigger!"

Luke took several steps onto the uneven tangle of packed snow, his hopes rising when he realized it had been a relatively small slide, only about a hundred feet wide and two hundred yards long. He looked around for anything dark, like a hat or glove or . . . anything. He cupped his hands to his mouth. "Camry!"

He stilled, listening. "Goddammit, Camry, answer me!"

But all he heard was terrifying silence.

"Okay, AuClair," he growled, stumbling to the center of the small avalanche field. "If you're my greatest ally, then help me find my miracle!"

Luke was trembling so badly that he had to stop, plant his feet, and rest his hands on his knees in an attempt to calm his racing heart. "Help me," he whispered, closing his eyes against his burning tears. "Show me where to look."

He suddenly held his breath, not moving a muscle when he heard a faint chirping sound. Still not breathing, he cocked his head one way and then the other.

There—just to his left: that unmistakable chirp of Podly's transmitter! The last he remembered seeing it, Camry had tucked it in her jacket pocket in order to read the note Roger had left him.

Could it still be in her pocket?

"Max! Come!" he called, taking several steps to the left and dropping to his knees. He grabbed the excited dog and held him still. "Listen."

And there it was again, a slightly louder chirp.

"Hear that, boy? Get the toy. Come on, dig up the toy!" he urged, driving his hands into the snow. "Dig, Max!"

They dug a hole at least three feet deep before Max suddenly lifted his head, a tiny wizard's hat in his mouth.

"Yes, you found Tigger!" Luke cried, digging frantically. If Tigger was here, there was a good chance Camry was with her.

His hand suddenly struck metal. "Camry!" he shouted. "Answer me!"

"Luke," came a muffled sound, making him still again.

"Camry!"

"Lu—"

He dug harder, working his way along the metal sled in each direction, until he felt the tarp. He pulled off his glove to wiggle his fingers under the canvas, and touched her jacket.

"I've got you!" he shouted. He had to shove Max out of the way when the dog tried to drive his nose into the narrow opening. "Keep digging, Max. Right here," he said, patting the snow toward the front of the sled.

While Max dug, Luke carefully worked more snow away from the tarp until he was able to peel it back enough to see inside. But all he could see was the red of Camry's jacket. He climbed out of the hole, knelt down on the opposite side, grabbed the edge of the tarp, and pulled with all his strength.

It slowly peeled back, revealing Camry's folded body wedged into the sled so tightly, he was afraid she couldn't breathe.

"Max, no!" Luke grabbed Max by the collar when the dog started nosing Camry's hair, dragged the Lab up out of the hole, and pushed him away.

Luke then straddled the hole, bracing his feet on either side of the sled. "Camry, sweetheart," he whispered, slipping off his glove again and carefully threading his trembling fingers through her hair. He felt along her jaw to locate her neck, then held his finger against her weak pulse. "Easy now," he said when she stirred with a moan. "Don't move. We don't know what's broken."

"Tigger," she said weakly, her voice muffled because her face was pressed into her knees, facing down.

"To hell with Tigger," he growled. "I need to know where you're hurt. Can you feel your body, Camry? Your legs? Your arms?"

"T-take Tig . . ." she whispered. "C-can't breathe."

Luke felt along her body, carefully wedging his fingers between her arm and torso, and finally realized that she was wrapped around the dachshund so tightly, there was no room for her lungs to expand. He pressed deeper until he felt Tigger's sweater, then grasped the wool and slowly pulled. Camry moaned again as the limp body of the dog slowly emerged. As soon as he was able to get both hands around Tigger, Luke applied more pressure while carefully wiggling the dog back and forth, then finally pulled the dachshund free and set her on the snow above the hole.

He immediately looked down at Camry and saw her stir again, her torso expanding on a shuddering breath. "Okay, sweetheart, your turn." He clasped the shoulder of her jacket, at the same time wrapping his hand around her neck to keep her head still, and leaned close. "If you feel any sharp pain, you let me know, okay? I'm going to pull you out now. Don't try to help; just relax and let me do all the work."

He put just enough pressure into his pull to gauge how stuck she was, then stilled, watching for signs of distress. He pulled a bit harder, felt her sliding free, then lifted her just a bit more before he stopped again. He then slid his arm under her head for support and repositioned his hand on her jacket. Using his own body like a backboard, he slowly straightened as she unfolded out of the sled, until he was leaning back against the side of the hole with her in front of him.

"Can you feel your legs and arms?" he whispered into her ear, which was now even with his head.

"Right leg h-hurts."

Luke was so relieved he kissed her hair. "That's good. You'd have really scared me if you said you couldn't feel anything. Okay," he said, taking a steadying breath to calm his trembling. "I'll straighten my knees so that I'm standing, then reach under your legs and lift you into my arms. There's a chance your right leg is broken, but I've got to lift you up and lay you on the snow." He kissed her hair again. "Ready?"

She made a small sound, and her head, which

he was still supporting, nodded ever so slightly. He reached down and cupped her legs—gritting his teeth against her gasp of pain—and lifted her to his chest. "Easy, now. The worst is over," he said softly, brushing his lips against her cold, tear-dampened cheek.

Careful not to fall into the sled, he slowly turned around, raised her up, and gently set her beside the hole. He slid his arms out from under her, making sure her body was completely supported by the snow.

"Tigger," she whispered, sucking in deep breaths.

"You first," he hissed, having to shove Max away when the whining dog started licking her face.

"Not breathing," Camry said, weakly giving Luke a push. "Please . . . help Tig."

He glanced over his shoulder at the dachshund's limp body. Dammit! "I think . . . I'm sorry, I think she's dead," he said, turning back to carefully unzip Camry's ski pants leg.

"P-please, Luke," she sobbed.

He spun around with a muttered curse, stepped across the hole, and leaned down to put his ear against Tigger's side. He thought he heard a faint heartbeat, and moved his face to her snout, trying to find signs of breathing.

"Help her," Camry whispered.

Luke slid two fingers under Tigger's sweater, over her ribs, then used his other hand to lift the dachshund's nose so he could close his mouth over it. He gently blew, feeling the dog's chest rise, then blew several more times. Tigger suddenly stirred, giving a weak whimper, and Luke picked up the dog.

"Come on, baby," he whispered, turning to show Camry. "Thatta girl. Keep breathing." He set Tigger on the snow in the crook of her arm, then took her hand to stop her from trying to pull the dog onto her chest. "Don't try to pick her up. Just let her lie beside you. She's breathing. Just keep her tucked against you."

He brushed back Camry's hair and leaned closer. "Anything else hurt besides your right leg? Your ribs? Your back?" he asked, unzipping her jacket. He stopped and blew on his hands to warm his freezing fingers, then slowly pulled her sweater up and worked the hem of her turtleneck out of her pants so he could feel her belly. "Focus on *yourself,* Camry," he growled when he glanced up to find her straining to see Tigger. He touched her chin to make her look at him, then forced a smile to soften his demand. "I'm worried about internal bleeding. Do you remember anything jabbing you as you tumbled? Or did your head hit anything?" he asked, studying her pupils, which, thank God, appeared even.

"I-I'm okay. B-but my foot is throbbing."

He forced his smile wider, brushing his shaking hand over her forehead again. "You picked a hell of a way to get out of your turn to pull the sled."

Her gaze roamed his face, and she touched his cheek. "You're bleeding."

He also touched his cheek, then smiled at her again. "I've known you what . . . two weeks? And I've been beaten up twice. You should come with a warning label."

"I'm sorry."

He kissed her trembling lips. "I'm not," he whispered. He straightened, then turned toward her legs. "Okay. Time to assess the damage."

Max suddenly came bounding over, dragging one of the snowshoes. "Good boy, Max!" Luke said, quickly grabbing it when the dog nearly swung the three-foot-long snowshoe into Camry. "You found my boot! Go on," he said. "Find more stuff, Max."

Tigger whined and started squirming. Luke caught the dachshund just as she started slipping into the hole he was standing in. "Looks like you're recovering okay," he said, setting the dog on her feet and holding her steady. He let her go as soon as he saw her tail wag, then shot Camry a glare. "You tell anyone I gave mouth-to-mouth resuscitation to a dog, and I'm going to post the cell phone picture I took of you in your wench's costume on the Web."

Before she could answer him, he moved back to finish unzipping the right leg of her ski pants. "I don't see any bones sticking out," he said with false joy—because he sure as hell saw that her foot was twisted at an unnatural angle.

He pulled out his multitool and opened the blade, then bobbed his eyebrows at her. "I've always fantasized about playing doctor on a beautiful woman." He looked back down at her leg. "I need to slit your inner pants and long johns from the knee down, to see what's happening in there." He bobbed his eyebrows again. "Assuming I can see anything, since you haven't shaved your legs in what . . . days?"

"Just *do* it," she growled, stiffening. "And tell me if it's broken or just sprained."

Oh, he knew it was broken, all right; he just didn't know how badly. He pulled her wool pants and long johns away from her leg and slit them open with his knife, exposing angry red skin swelling up from under her wool sock.

"Yup, it's broken," he muttered, carefully cutting the sock down to her boot. He stilled when she sucked in a hiss, and looked at her. "I can't tell if it's your lower leg or your ankle. I have to take off your boot, Camry. I'll do it as gently as I can."

"Leave it on."

"No. Your foot's swelling, and it's only going to get worse."

She closed her eyes. "Then do it."

Luke carefully sliced her laces, then set down the knife in order to peel open her boot, wincing when she hissed again. "Easy now," he crooned, lifting back the tongue of her boot. He slid one hand under her ankle, then grabbed the heel of the boot and slowly pulled.

"No, stop!"

He stilled, turning to see her take several gulping breaths before she gritted her teeth. "Okay. Do it."

He held his own breath as he started pulling again, working as quickly as he could so he wouldn't prolong her agony while being careful he didn't do any more damage. The boot finally slipped free, taking her sock with it, and Luke closed his eyes. "I think your ankle is shattered," he whispered. He looked over at her. "No blood, though. So I'll just immobilize it as best I can. Then I'm digging out the sled, and we'll get you to a hospital lickety-split. Where's the closest house to here?"

She thought for a moment. "If we go down the

tote road about ten miles, then cut across the bay, I think there are some year-round homes out on the point."

Luke's gut tightened. "Do you think the bay is frozen solid?"

"I-it should be."

He glanced down at her ankle then back at her, and shook his head. "It's not a life-threatening injury, Camry, as long as you don't go into shock. So I'd rather not risk our drowning to save some miles. How far to your sister's house? Doesn't she live on this side of the bay?"

"Maybe eighteen or twenty miles from here."

Luke gently laid her foot on the open leg of her ski pants and turned in the hole he'd been standing in the whole time. "If I can find the other snowshoe, I can get us there by midnight." He got down on his knees and started rummaging around in the sled. He pulled out the sleeping bag and straw mattress, but didn't see the rest of their gear. "The gear must have broken free," he said, straightening with the sleeping bag, which he unrolled and laid over her. "I'll try to find it. I'd like to at least have the headlamp for when it gets dark, and the first-aid kit."

"How did you know where to dig for me?" she asked, helping him tuck the bag around her.

He grabbed the small mattress and tucked the

corner of it under her shoulders. But before he lowered her head, he kissed her gently on the lips with a soft chuckle. "That damn transmitter started beeping, and Max and I followed the sound."

She blinked up at him. "I don't have the transmitter," she whispered. "I-I threw it out onto the lake this morning, when I decided to . . . to see things your way," she said.

"You threw it away? But I heard it. Max heard it, too. It's how we found you!"

"That's impossible, Luke." She reached under the sleeping bag. "I don't have it anymore." She suddenly gasped, and her hand reappeared holding the transmitter. "Oh my God," she whispered, holding it toward him. "H-how is that possible?"

Luke damn near started laughing hysterically when the tiny instrument suddenly gave a lively chirp. He took the transmitter from her and studied it. "This thing keeps turning up like a bad penny." He looked at her. "It shouldn't even have its own power source, so what in hell keeps making that noise?"

She turned her head away. "I have no idea."

He gently turned her face to look at him. "Don't try to live by my beliefs, Camry, at the expense of your own," he softly told her. "I was wrong to pretend to go along with you and AuClair instead of telling you I thought it was all an act." He held the transmitter up for her to see. "But this *infernal thing*," he said with a crooked smile, "seems determined to make me believe." He shoved it in his pocket, kissed her again, then climbed out of the hole.

He freed his boot from the snowshoe Max had found, sat down and put it on, then crawled over and lifted the edge of the sleeping bag off her right foot. "It's still swelling," he said, carefully covering her foot again. "I'm going to hunt for our gear before I immobilize it. I'd like to find the first-aid kit, because I tossed what was left of our pain pills in it. Are you comfortable enough?"

"I'm okay. Where's Tigger?"

"She seems to be fully recovered, and is nosing the snow with Max. I'm giving myself twenty minutes to search, and then we're out of here, gear or no gear. Just close your eyes and rest. I'm afraid you might be in for a painful afternoon."

"I'm sorry. I wish I could help you."

He chuckled. "If you want to help, then picture our snowcat magically appearing while I go to work on my own miracle."

Chapter Twenty

$\mathcal{A}$s "seemingly impossible tasks" went, Luke decided this one was a doozy. Getting back to civilization had appeared daunting enough when they'd both been hale and hearty, but getting Camry out of these woods with a broken ankle—without killing her in the process—might very well prove impossible.

Unless . . .

Luke shoved his hand in his pocket and touched the transmitter. How in hell did the damn thing keep turning up just when they needed it? He believed Camry when she said she'd thrown it away this morning—just as he had the other day, when he'd smashed it into that tree and watched it shatter into a hundred pieces. Yet here it was again, and they'd *both* heard it chirping just now.

Max had heard it, too. And dogs didn't know anything about miracles, did they?

Luke walked toward a dark spot in the snow and thought about Maxine's determination to rescue both Kate and him at the expense of his own life. If the fact was that Maxine had shown up at the pound just hours before they'd taken Kate over to pick out a dog, or that a five-year-old had seen something in the mangy old mutt that none of the adults had, was that the beginning of a miracle, or merely a string of sequential coincidences?

But then, did it matter *what* it was, as long as everything had turned out okay?

Well, except for Maxine.

Luke stopped suddenly and stared down at what looked like Roger AuClair's large pointed hat lying in the snow. Where in hell had that come from? Had it been in the sled all this time, and he just hadn't noticed? If Camry had found it, she certainly wouldn't have shown it to him, now, would she? Not after learning what he thought of AuClair's hocus-pocus.

Which she wholeheartedly embraced.

Maybe the question he should be asking was, If the magic really *did* rule science, could it be manipulated?

Even by a nonbeliever who was just desperate enough to try?

Luke looked around and saw Max and Tigger digging in the snow several yards away, apparently having discovered something worth salvaging. He looked at Camry and saw her lying quietly, her arm over her face to shield out the sun.

"How are you doing over there?" he called to her.

"I'm fine," she called back, not moving, "as long as I don't move."

Luke dropped his gaze to the hat, took a deep breath, and picked it up.

Something fell out of it. He bent over again, and picked up what appeared to be the card Roger had left for him. He opened it, scanned what Camry had already read to him, then continued from where she'd left off.

If you're harboring any dark thoughts that I had anything to do with the predicament you're in, Renoir, then think again. Free will dictates circumstances, not the magic. Life is a fragile gift, and if you can't embrace it all—the good, the bad, and the ugly—then you might as well stop breathing, since this is an all or nothing thing.

So the answer to your question is yes; just like your numbers, the magic can be manipulated. I was telling it straight the other day, when I told Camry that everyone has the power within them to create.

That is, assuming it's a creation of the heart.

The only brick walls people run into are of their own making. Take this particular brick wall, for instance, that you are right now trying to figure a way around. If I might be so bold as to suggest . . . why don't you take your own advice that you gave Camry, and simply go through it? You have the power to do that by merely turning off your analytical brain long enough to hear what your heart is telling you. I believe you'll find that when you do, what you consider obstacles might actually work to your advantage.

If you need more time, then stop the clock. And if you want to ease Camry's pain, then find a way. It's a simple matter of deciding what you need to happen, then acting as if it already has.

Miracles are really more about perception than actual fact. If all you see are obstacles, you'll be taking two steps back for every step forward; but if you can see the magic in them, you'll realize those obstacles might be blessings in disguise.

So the choice is yours, Renoir. Your logic can take you only so far, and if you want to get Camry home, you're going to have to rely on what your heart tells you to do. Just think back thirteen years, Luke, and ask yourself if you haven't already experienced what it is to create a miracle.

I'm afraid there's one other decision you're going to have to make before this is over, however, which will require a true leap of faith. But I'm hoping that by the time you have to make it, it will be a no-brainer—no pun intended, Doctor.

You see, Camry has an aunt who can heal her in a rather . . . well, let's call it an unconventional way, shall we? Libby MacBain will be at Gù Brath celebrating the solstice with everyone, so you might want to consider heading directly there, rather than wasting precious time trying to get Camry to a hospital and risk her never walking properly again.

"Goddammit, AuClair," Luke growled, glaring down at the card. "You almost had me up to this point, you old bastard. An aunt who can magically heal her ankle," he muttered, wiping a hand over his face.

"Did you find the first-aid kit, Luke?" Camry called to him. "One of those pills would be nice right about now."

Christ, what was he doing, reading some crazy old man's rantings! He crumpled the card and tossed it in the snow, along with Roger's stupid hat. "I think Max and Tigger have dug something up," he called out, running to the dogs. "What have you two found?" he asked, using his anger at himself to sound excited for them.

He edged Tigger out of the way, reached down into the shallow hole, and gave a tug on the material they'd unearthed. "Camry, they found our bag of gear!" He scrambled to his feet. "Okay, guys," he said, slapping his leg. "Come on. Now let's go find my other snowshoe!"

He walked over and knelt beside Camry, then picked up the snowshoe Max had found earlier and held it out to the dogs, letting them sniff it. "See this? Find the other snowshoe, and I'll make you each a whole pot of soup tonight."

They cocked their heads back and forth, listening to him, then both suddenly shot off in opposite directions. Luke smiled down at Camry. "If they come back with that snowshoe, I'm going to have to stop calling them simple beasts." He opened the bag and dug through their gear to find the first-aid kit. "Have you figured out yet if you're hurt anywhere else?" he asked, opening the kit and scanning the contents. He grew alarmed when she didn't answer. "What else hurts?"

"I think I may have cracked some ribs," she whispered, her eyes filled with pain. "I can breathe okay, so my lung isn't punctured or anything. But what if riding in the sled finishes breaking one of my ribs?"

Luke closed his eyes.

She touched his arm. "Maybe you should go for help alone. You can move me to the trees, build a fire, and the dogs can stay with me. You'll make better time if you don't have to tow me in the sled. Then Life Flight can fly me out."

"I'm not leaving you. If something were to happen to me, nobody knows you're out here."

"Daddy knows. We stole his groomer, remember?"

"But it might be days before he starts looking for us." He shook his head. "I'm not leaving you," he repeated. "We make it out together or we die trying—*together*."

He returned to scanning the kit, then pulled out the pills. "These should help," he said, opening the bottle. He pulled out one of the bottles of water they'd melted this morning, popped a pill in her mouth, then held her head for her to drink. "Okay, I'm going to dig out the sled while we give that pill time to kick in."

"Luke," she said, grabbing his sleeve when he started to stand up. "What were you doing a few minutes ago, when you were just standing up there? It looked as if you were reading something."

"I found AuClair's card, and was reading from where you'd left off."

"Anything interesting?" she asked, her eyes searching his.

He stood up. "Not really. Just more philosophical bunk about how I can make a miracle happen just by deciding I want one." He shrugged. "He even said I have the power to stop time, if I just put my mind to it. No, not my mind," he muttered, sliding into the hole beside her. He gave a forced smile. "He said I had to turn off my analytical brain, and think with my heart. Close your eyes, Camry," he said, not wanting to deal with the hopefulness he saw shining in them. "Relax and let that pill work."

With a muttered curse at the wounded look she gave him before she turned her head and closed her eyes, Luke also turned away and went to work on the sled. It took him about ten minutes to dig it out, and another ten minutes to straighten a bent ski and make it snow worthy again. He'd just finished tying their gear to the back when Tigger came trotting over, the GPS in her mouth. Luke felt in his pocket, realizing it must have fallen out during the avalanche.

"Good girl, Tig!" he said, roughing up the hair on her head. "I take back every bad thing I've thought about you. You and your buddy Max are a hell of a lot smarter than many people I know." He kissed the top of her head. "And I'm going to buy you a whole wardrobe of pretty sweaters."

Apparently not wanting to be outdone, Max came trotting over dragging the other snowshoe. Luke sat back on his heels. The dogs had actually found everything he needed? He shook his head in disbelief, wondering how they seemed to know how desperate the situation was.

"Okay, you pooches. You've definitely earned your soup—as well as a couple of hero medals, which I am personally going to see that you get."

They suddenly took off again in search of more treasure. Luke turned to show Camry what they'd found, but she was asleep. Lifting the edge of the sleeping bag, he actually winced when he saw how swollen her ankle was.

"Camry, honey," he said softly, gentling shaking her shoulder. "I need you to be awake while I immobilize your foot, so I know if I'm doing anything wrong."

Her eyes dark with drugged confusion and pain, she nodded.

Luke moved back down her leg. But just as he lifted the sleeping bag again, the dogs came bounding back, each carrying something. Only instead of bringing their newest finds to him, they brought them to Camry.

Max dropped the large pointed hat on her chest, and Tigger dropped the crumpled card. Then both dogs lay down, Max resting his chin on her belly and Tigger curling up beside her shoulder.

Luke sighed. Was he ever going to get rid of

Roger AuClair? "Here's an idea," he said, folding the sleeping bag back to expose her ankle. "You can finish reading Roger's letter to me while I play doctor on you." He shot her a smile. "And why don't you put on his hat, and try to sound just like him."

Her eyes filled with tears, and her chin quivered. "D-don't humor me, Luke."

"No! I'm not humoring you, I'm trying to distract you. And myself. Here," he said, uncrumpling the card and handing it to her. "Okay, let's hear what other sage advice good old Roger has for me." He arched an eyebrow. "Maybe at the end of the note, he tells us where he stashed the snowcat."

Probably as much from her own curiosity as wishing to humor *him,* Camry hesitantly started reading out loud from where she'd left off yesterday morning. Using the laces he'd stolen from her other boot, and a pair of pants he'd taken from their gear, Luke carefully started to wrap her ankle.

He paused when she stopped reading with a hiss of pain. "Sorry. I'm trying to be gentle. Go on, keep reading."

"But Roger said there's a chance I might never walk properly again," she whispered, her chin quivering again. "Luke, you have to do what he says, and take me straight to my aunt Libby. She's really a highly skilled trauma surgeon, but she also has a gift for healing people by only touching them."

"You won't just be walking properly, you'll be running a marathon by this summer," he said, giving her arm a squeeze. "Keep going. You've reached the part where I stopped reading."

Her eyes searched his, looking for . . . hell, for some sign he believed her, Luke figured. He went back to work on her foot, wrapping several layers of the heavy pant material around her leg, from her knee to down past her heel. He then gently tied it in place, careful not to make it too tight around the swelling.

He heard her take a shuddering breath; then she started reading again.

I warned you this was going to seem impossible, Renoir. But making a miracle is actually the easy part, whereas living with the realization that you really are in control of your own destiny is what's truly daunting.

So I wish you the best of luck, young man—not only on your immediate journey, but on your life's journey as well. Now don't you go feeling bad that I left before you got to thank me for all I've done for you; we'll be meeting again one day, so you'll get your chance. Godspeed, Renoir. Your faithful servant, Roger de Keage.

Luke snorted. "If we meet again, I'll likely wring his neck."

"My God," she whispered. "He's the father of the clan MacKeage."

"The father of practical jokes, you mean," he muttered.

"Um . . . there's a P.S."

Luke snorted again. "The old bastard does love to pontificate."

She dropped her worried gaze back to the card. "P.S.," she read. *"You're down to six hours and forty-four minutes, Renoir, so you might want to get cracking on making that miracle."*

Chapter Twenty-one

Four hours later, Luke was worried that instead of saving Camry's life, he very well might be killing her. For the third time in half an hour, he dropped to his knees beside the sled, utterly exhausted from the grueling pace he'd set, and peeled back the tarp. Tigger blinked up at him from inside Camry's jacket with a mournful whine, then gently lapped her pale cheek before looking at Luke again.

"I know, Tig," he said between ragged breaths as he took off his gloves. He reached in and touched Camry's neck, feeling her faint pulse, which had grown steadily fainter in the last four hours. "I'm worried about her, too.

You're doing a good job of keeping her warm,"
he crooned, sliding his hand under the jacket
to make sure the dog's weight was still on the
mattress, and not putting pressure on Camry's
ribs. He rubbed Tigger's ear. "Let's hope it's the
extra pill I gave her that's making her sleep, and
not shock."

He wrapped his arm around Max when the
dog came over and nosed Camry, also whining
worriedly. "Okay, gang, we need to come up with
a new game plan," he whispered, his hand trembling as he patted Max. "Because this one isn't
working."

Max drove his nose inside the sled beside Camry's body, then lifted his head with Roger's pointed
hat in his mouth and dropped the hat on her face.
When Luke quickly snatched it off, Max nosed
Camry's hair with a whine.

"Okay, if it will make you feel better, I'll put it
on her," Luke said, carefully replacing the wool
hat she was wearing with the heavy velvet pointed
one.

Camry stirred, and two faint flags of color appeared on her cheeks.

Luke touched his finger to her pulse again
and found it much stronger. "Whoa," he whispered on an indrawn breath. "That certainly
helped." He glanced at Max, then at Tigger. "Any

other suggestions? Because at this point I'm open to anything, no matter how harebrained it might sound."

Max suddenly took off down the road, then just as suddenly veered into the woods. He stopped, looked back at Luke, and started barking.

Luke stood up, groaning when his muscles protested, and closed the tarp back over the sled. "Come on, Tig. Let's go see where Max thinks he's going," he muttered, hooking the rope back over his shoulders and starting off down the road.

But he suddenly picked up his pace with renewed hope. Maybe Max smelled a wood fire or something else that meant that help was close by.

When he reached the spot where the Lab had gone into the woods, Luke found what looked like a game trail. Max was standing about twenty yards in, facing him, his tail wagging. He barked again, then took off deeper into the woods.

Luke glanced down the road—the certain path to civilization—then back toward where Max had disappeared, trying to see through the trees. The sun had dropped below the horizon already, even though it wasn't even four o'clock. Today was the shortest day of the year, and Luke knew that he was facing the longest night of the year. But even in what little light that was left, he could see that the lake was about a hundred yards from where he was standing.

Out of sight now, Max started barking excitedly.

Luke looked back down the road. He didn't want to expend his energy on a wild-goose chase, but he didn't want to walk right past help, either.

Tigger suddenly jumped out of the sled and started lunging through the deep snow right past him, following Max's path.

"I guess that settles that," he muttered, stepping back to check on Camry. When he saw she was looking far less pale than she had been, he turned and started following the dogs. The trail emerged onto the shoreline, and Luke stopped beside Max and Tigger, who were looking out at the lake, their wagging tails brushing the snow.

Luke pulled his GPS out of his pocket, called up the screen that told him exactly where he was, and realized that he was still sixteen miles from Winter's house by way of the tote road. A chill ran down his spine as he recalled Roger's note; it appeared he *had* been taking two steps back for each step forward.

They had traveled only two miles in four hours.

Which meant that at the rate he was

walking—which was only going to get slower the more tired he grew—it was going to take him days to get them out of these woods. He zoomed out the map on the screen and saw that if he cut diagonally down the lake, Pine Creek was less than six miles away.

Of flat going.

With a full moon to light the way.

And possibly thin ice that he wouldn't be able to see.

Did he have the right to risk drowning Camry . . . to save her foot?

But it wasn't really her ankle that worried him; he was afraid she was going into shock. And though he didn't know much about medicine—emergency or otherwise—he was pretty sure shock was fatal if not treated in time.

He stepped to the sled and peeled back the tarp, plopped down in the snow and took off his glove, then reached in and wrapped his fingers around Camry's hand. He looked back out at the expanse of lake in front of him. Could he really shut down his brain long enough to follow his heart?

Just like he had thirteen years ago, when he'd found Kate and Maxine?

He hadn't stopped long enough to weigh the odds of his saving Kate versus their drowning.

Hell, he hadn't been thinking at all; he'd just acted on instinct. Nothing had mattered except getting her away from that river, and if they'd both drowned, well . . . he would have died knowing she hadn't died alone.

But by some miracle, neither of them had.

Was that what Roger had meant in his note, when he'd written that Luke had already experienced creating a miracle when he'd needed it?

Because honest to God, from when he'd found Kate's and Maxine's tracks under that tree to when he'd gone out onto the ice sheet after them, it had felt like time had actually stopped. He'd reached the river in what had seemed like only seconds, even though it had been over a mile away, then taken off his snowshoes, gone out to her, and flung her to safety with absolutely no sense of urgency. His actions hadn't been rushed or even in slow motion; time had truly ceased to exist.

So why in hell was he so determined to deny that miracles existed?

Because if they did exist, it would mean there really was some unknown factor ruling his beloved science, something that he couldn't quantify . . . or control.

And God knows he'd spent his entire pre-adult life feeling out of control—from his accidental conception and arrival into the world, to his being raised by three women determined to mother him, to his mother's marriage to a man who had been equally determined to father him. Even getting a baby sister he hadn't asked for.

So maybe the real miracle on that river had absolutely nothing to do with Kate, but rather with the fact that, for the first time in his life, he'd stopped being self-centered long enough to uncompromisingly, unpretentiously, and unconditionally love someone other than himself.

A condition that had lasted all of four weeks, until he'd returned to school and fallen right back into his old habit of putting himself first. And he'd tenaciously clung to his self-centeredness all through his career, not collaborating with anyone unless it served him more than it served the greater good, and even going so far as to steal someone else's work when he'd lost control of his own.

Christ, he deserved to die out here.

But Camry sure as hell didn't—because she loved him *exactly the way he was*.

And he sure as hell loved her more than he loved himself.

So maybe it *was* time he listened to his heart.

Luke looked at his watch and saw it was four o'clock. He lifted Camry's hand and kissed the stone ring on her finger, then tucked it back under the sleeping bag, got to his knees, and kissed her warm forehead.

"Okay, sleeping beauty," he whispered. "It's time for me to make some magic." He snuggled Roger's hat farther down on her head. "Too bad you're going to sleep right through the miracle I'm about to create."

He stood up, picked up Tigger, and tucked her back inside Camry's jacket. Then, after removing the bag of gear from the back of the sled and tossing it in the snow, he patted his leg. "Come on, Max. You're riding, too." He set the Lab in the sled, making sure the dog didn't crowd Camry and Tigger. "Santa Claus is arriving at Gù Brath on the solstice this year, and I'm the reindeer who's going to make this sled fly. So hang on tight, everyone," he finished with a laugh, closing the tarp and securing it to the side.

He stepped to the front of the sled, settled the rope over his shoulders, then reached into his pockets for his gloves. After putting them on, he pulled the GPS out of one pocket and the transmitter out of the other.

Luke tossed the GPS in the snow next to their gear, then held up the transmitter. "Okay, Rudolph, you guide my sleigh to Camry's house, because her mother's expecting her daughter to blow out thirty-two candles in a two hours and fifteen minutes."

The infernal thing gave a lively chirp.

Luke tucked it in his pocket with a laugh, then stepped out onto the lake. He took another step, and then another, keeping pace with the soft chirps coming from his pocket.

Chapter Twenty-two

So deep was Luke in the zone of putting one foot in front of the other that it took him a moment to realize that something was interfering with his hearing the steady chirp of the transmitter. He looked up from the moonlit snow in front of him and stopped dead in his tracks.

Max started yipping, and Luke shrugged off the rope and went back and opened the tarp. The Lab immediately jumped out and ran toward the bright lights of town, barking frantically. Luke peered in to see that Camry was still sleeping, her relaxed face rosy pink as Tigger's wagging tail made her jacket move. He petted the dachshund. "You did good, girl. You've kept her toasty warm. Hang on, we're almost there."

Luke closed the tarp and started after Max, soon walking up over the shoreline, past the shops, and directly onto Main Street. He then held up his hand to stop the pickup slowing down to let him cross.

But instead of crossing the road, he walked to the driver's window. "I need a ride to TarStone Mountain Ski Resort," he said when the driver rolled down his window. He gestured toward the sled. "My wife is injured. Could you please give us a lift?"

The man put the truck in park and got out, only nearly to trip over Luke's snowshoes. "Sure," he said, going to the sled and pushing Max out of the way to fold back the tarp. He suddenly reared upright. "Hell, that's Camry MacKeage," he said, spinning back toward Luke. "You say she's your *wife*?"

Luke tossed his snowshoes into the bed of the truck and walked over and pulled the tarp completely off. "You got a problem with that?" he asked, lifting Tigger out of her jacket and shoving the dog into the man's arms.

The man grinned. "No, sir. But I certainly do wish you luck." He nodded toward the sled. "Camry wrenched my brother's knee during a brawl at my bar about six months ago." After shifting Tigger to one arm, he held out his hand. "Pete Johnson."

Luke shook his hand. "Luke Renoir. So, Pete, does that mean you're not going to give us a lift?"

"Oh, jeez, no," he said with a laugh. "My brother deserved both the wrenched knee and the scathing lecture I gave him once he sobered up. Come on," he said, opening the back door of the crew cab to set Tigger inside. He motioned for Max to jump in, then walked back to the sled. "Jeez, she must be hurt bad if she's not waking up," he said, just as Luke straightened with Camry in his arms. "Hold your damn horses!" he shouted at the car behind them when the driver honked his horn. He rushed around to open the passenger's-side door. "What's the matter with her?"

"She has a broken ankle and maybe a couple of cracked ribs," Luke told him, gently setting Camry on the seat and sliding her to the middle. He crawled in beside her, then tucked her under his arm and laid her bundled right leg over his own. "Could you just pull the sled to the side-walk? I'll come back and pick it up later."

Pete closed the door, ran to the sled, picked it up, and tossed it in the bed of his truck, then climbed in behind the wheel. "If she's got a bro-ken ankle, I better drive you to the hospital in Greenville," he said, putting the truck in gear.

"No, I need to get her home before she goes into total shock. She has an aunt there who's a trauma specialist, who can help her while we call for an ambulance."

"Libby MacBain," Pete said. "I know her, and yeah, that's probably a good idea. Doc Libby's kept more than one person alive while waiting for an ambulance." He glanced over at Luke, then back at the road. "What happened? Was it a snowmobile accident or something? You look like you've been walking awhile."

"Avalanche," Luke said, setting his finger over Camry's pulse, sighing in relief when he felt it beating steady and strong.

"An avalanche? That's rare in these parts. Where'd it happen?"

"Just south of Springy Mountain."

Pete glanced over at him in surprise. "You hauled her all the way here in that makeshift sled? Down the *lake*?" He looked back at the road, shaking his head. "You either got more balls than brains, or one hell of a guardian angel." He glanced at Luke again. "The lake ain't frozen over in places, you know."

"Apparently the last six miles of it are."

Pete turned onto the TarStone Mountain Ski Resort road. "What's up with the funny hat?" he asked.

Luke settled it farther down on Camry's head. "It's a birthday gift from a relative."

"Oh yeah, that's right. Today's the MacKeage girls' birthday." He snorted. "Hell of a way for a woman to spend her birthday." He glanced at Luke again. "Talk in town when Camry was here last summer was that she didn't even have a boyfriend. How long you two been married?"

"A couple of days."

Pete chuckled humorlessly. "Hell of a way to spend a honeymoon, too. But I suppose honeymooning in the mountains in the middle of the winter, instead of on some warm beach in the Caribbean, ain't all that far-fetched for Camry." He turned off the road just as the resort came into sight, and pulled up into the driveway of Gù Brath. He stopped in front of the bridge leading to the front door, then shut off the truck with a sigh as he looked directly at Luke. "The MacKeages are pillars of the community, but they're . . . um . . . a bit on the strange side. They're a tight-knit clan, along with the MacBains." He opened his door, then shot Luke a grin. "I had a thing for Cam's older sister Heather when we were in high school, but her daddy scared the bejeezus out of me so bad, I never dared to ask her out. You need help getting Cam inside?" he asked, glancing at the well-lit house.

"No, I've got her," Luke said, opening his door. "If you can just bring the dogs."

"I'll let them out, and they can follow you in." He glanced at the house again, and Luke would have sworn the man shivered. "I got to get down to my bar. We open at five, and the staff is waiting for me."

Luke stilled just as he was getting ready to get out, and lifted his wrist.

Holy hell, his watch said four fifteen!

A vehicle pulled up behind them, doors opened and closed, and a man and woman walked up to Luke's side of the truck and peered in his open door.

"Oh my God, Camry!" gasped the woman holding the young toddler. "Robbie, take her. She's hurt."

"No, I've got her," Luke said, carefully sliding out of the truck with Camry in his arms, then shouldering past the tall man. "Thanks for your help, Pete," he called out as he strode onto the bridge. "I'll catch up with you later."

The man named Robbie rushed ahead and opened the door.

"Could you make sure the dogs come in?" Luke asked, stepping inside the foyer, the sounds of voices and playing children assaulting his senses. He stopped and looked around, blinking against the blast of hot air that made his eyes water, and even stepped back when several people rushed up to him.

"Camry!" someone cried. "Mom! Dad! Camry's here, and she's hurt!"

Another man stepped forward and reached out to take her, but Luke took another step back. "No, I've got her. Is her aunt Libby here?"

"Libby's my mother," Robbie said from behind him, placing a hand on Luke's back and guiding him toward the living room. "She should be here soon. Why don't you lay Cam down on the couch?"

Luke walked into the living room, but instead of laying her down, he sat with Camry in his arms, then carefully stretched her right leg out on the couch beside him.

"What's wrong with her?" asked one of the women.

"She has a broken ankle and maybe some cracked ribs." Luke unzipped her jacket, but quickly reached out when the woman tried to take off Camry's hat. "No, that stays on until Libby MacBain gets here."

The sea of people crowding around them suddenly parted. "Camry!" Grace cried, dropping to her knees in front of Luke. She touched Camry's cheek, then looked up and smiled at Luke, her eyes shining with tears. "You brought her home," she whispered, reaching up and touching his beard. "Th-thank you."

Greylen MacKeage edged past his wife and reached out as if he intended to take Camry into his arms. Luke pulled her against him. "No, I've got her."

"She's hurt," Greylen growled.

"Leave her, Grey," Grace said gently, caressing Camry's cheek again. "She's in very good hands, and she's going to be okay."

"What happened?" Grey asked, kneeling beside his wife and touching Camry's cheek himself. He glared at Luke. "Did ye crash the snowcat? Why won't she wake up? Does she have a concussion?" he asked, reaching to remove her hat.

Luke held it in place. "It stays on until her aunt gets here," he repeated. "And we got caught in a small avalanche, and her ankle is shattered. Libby MacBain will heal her," he said, somewhat defiantly.

Greylen snapped his gaze to Luke in surprise. "Ye know," he whispered.

"I know," Luke said with a nod. "And just so *you* know, she's my wife."

"I don't remember giving my permission, Renoir."

Luke grinned tightly. "A distant relative of yours gave it for you."

Greylen arched one brow. "And just who would that be?"

"Roger AuClair."

He frowned. "I don't know anyone named Roger AuClair."

"No? Then how about Roger de Keage?"

Greylen reared back, his sharp green eyes narrowing. "Ye met de Keage?"

Luke nodded toward Camry. "That's his hat." He grinned again. "And he thanks you for the snowcat he said you would want him to have."

"Aunt Libby's here," someone said.

The people who'd crowded around them again moved out of the way, and a slender woman in her sixties leaned over Grace's shoulder to touch Camry's forehead.

She stood silently for several seconds, then lifted her eyes to Luke and smiled. "You got her here just in time. Robbie," she said, motioning him over, "carry her up to her room for me, would you?"

"No, I've got her," Luke said, leaning forward to stand up.

"Let Robbie take her," Greylen ordered. "Ye look like you can barely walk."

"*I've got her,*" Luke growled, levering himself

off the couch to his feet. He fell into step behind Grace, who led the way through the sea of people to the stairs.

"Ye drop her, Renoir, and ye better hope you break your own neck in the fall," Greylen said, walking beside him.

"Oh, quit posturing, Grey," Grace said with a laugh, turning to loop her arm through her husband's and pulling him up beside her. "She's not your daughter anymore, she's Luke's wife."

"It wasn't a legal marriage," Grey muttered.

"No? Then would you care to lay odds that when we check at the courthouse tomorrow morning, we won't find their license duly registered?" she asked.

"Pendaär is supposed to marry our girls."

Grace laughed again. "I'm sure Daar will defer to Roger de Keage."

If Luke hadn't been seconds away from falling to his knees, he was sure he'd have found their conversation intriguing. But he was so exhausted, he just wanted to see Camry open her eyes and smile at him so he could fall into a coma for a week. They reached the balcony, and he followed Grace and Greylen down the hall as Libby MacBain walked beside him. She reached out and quietly took hold of his elbow, and in less than three steps his exhaustion vanished and he suddenly felt like he could run a marathon.

He stopped and looked down at her.

"You have amazing endurance, Luke," she said, smiling up at him. "And a powerfully strong and rather *loud* heart."

"Yeah," he said, feeling a bit drunk from the sudden surge of energy coursing through him. "And every so often, I can actually *hear* it."

Chapter Twenty-three

"Can you ever forgive me?" Cam whispered against her father's chest, snuggled up in his arms on her bed.

Her mother, lying with her arms around both of them, squeezed her tightly. "We forgave you one second after Luke told us."

Her father's arms also tightened, and his lips brushed her hair. "Actually, we forgave you before we even knew, daughter, because we love you." He ducked his head to see her face. "You are supposed to come to us when you're having a crisis."

Cam sighed, closing her eyes with a smile, and snuggled deeper into his embrace to prepare for the coming lecture.

"But even though you should have," her mother rushed to say, apparently hoping to waylay her husband's scolding, "it soon became obvious to your father and me that Luke would be able to help you better than we could."

"It did?" her papa muttered.

"Yes," Grace said. "That's why instead of going to Go Back Cove to get you himself, your father thought it would be better to send Luke."

"I did?" He sighed, smoothing down Cam's hair. "I am such a wise man."

"So, oh wise father," Cam said with a giggle, "did you know you were sending my future husband to fetch me, or were you just hoping that by waving him in front of my nose, I would fall madly in love because he's big and strong and handsome and smart . . . just like you?"

His arms around her tightened. "Your falling in love with him was your mother's idea. Whereas I was perfectly content for you to remain a spinster your whole life."

Cam snorted, then turned her head to look at her mom. "I . . . we couldn't find Podly's data bank. I'm afraid it might be gone for good."

Grace patted her arm and sat up. "Maybe. But you and Luke don't really need it, do you?" she asked, getting off the bed and turning back with a smile. "With your combined brainpower, I'm sure you'll duplicate my work in no time, once you lock yourselves in my lab."

Cam also tried to sit up, but she seemed to be stuck in her father's embrace. She patted his chest and grinned up at him. "I'm not going far," she whispered.

When he reluctantly opened his arms, she jumped off the bed, then turned back to him. "Except that I do have to take a quick trip to British Columbia, to meet Luke's parents and sister. But we'll be back right after Christmas."

"I'm afraid that if you're going to British Columbia, you're going to miss them," Grace said. "Because they're here."

"They're *here*? But how did you know to invite them?"

Grace walked to the bathroom door and waved her over. "Come on, you need a bath. The party starts in less than an hour. And to answer your question, it seems Luke's mom got a card in the mail, inviting them all to Gù Brath for Christmas." Her eyes shone with amusement. "When his mother called to question me about the invitation, she mentioned the card had a beautiful angel on the front, and was signed by a flourished *F.*"

"Oh my God," Cam said, covering her mouth with her hands. "She sent Luke's family a card, too?"

"Would ye happen to know who F is?" her father asked, getting off the bed.

Cam looked from one parent to the other. "Um . . . it's Fiona."

Grey arched a brow. "*Our* Fiona?"

Cam sighed. "It's a long story, Papa. I'll tell you about my rather interesting last couple of weeks tomorrow, okay? I'm just dying to sink into a tub of hot water." She looked at her mother. "Where's Luke's family now?"

Grace started filling the tub, pouring a liberal amount of lilac-scented bath beads into the cascading water. "I imagine Kate pounced on Luke the moment he stepped out of his own shower. That girl is positively enchanting." She pulled Camry into her arms and kissed her on the forehead. "Welcome home, daughter of mine. I've never missed you so much as I did when I realized you really were missing."

"But now I'm found," Cam whispered back, hugging her tightly. "Fiona and Luke and Roger AuClair helped me find myself." She leaned away. "And . . . and you, Mama. You were always right there in my heart, guiding me every step of the way."

Cam turned when her father walked into the bathroom, and threw herself at him. "And you, too, Papa," she cried. "I could almost hear you lecturing me, letting me know how much you love me."

He squeezed her so tight she squeaked. "Sorry. I'm afraid you'll get no more lectures from me. That's your husband's duty now."

Cam looked up. "But Luke's not very good at it, Papa. He actually tried once, and my ears didn't even come close to falling off. In fact, I fell asleep."

He hugged her to him with a laugh, then kissed the top of her head. "I will see what I can do to remedy that. Welcome home, my precious highlander."

Chapter Twenty-four

Luke sat in the huge dining room of Gù Brath, more than a little overwhelmed and utterly awed by the sheer magnitude of the festivities. The boisterous younger children—whom Luke had heard more than one person refer to as little heathens—had temporarily been relegated to the playroom downstairs, apparently to give the adults a few minutes of peace. But there still had to be forty people—sitting and standing around the table, which was thirty feet long if it was a foot, and crammed in among the balloons and streamers—and every damn one of them was wearing a birthday hat.

Except him.

And Tigger.

At Camry's somewhat threatening insistence, Luke was wearing *AuClair's* hat, and Tigger was wearing her own miniature version.

Kate's snickering wasn't at all helping his mood, nor were her repeated requests that he look at her; each time he complied she would then take his picture on her cell phone.

Luke figured several of them were already posted on the Internet.

While they waited for Winter, who seemed to be late for her own birthday party, Luke tried to concentrate on putting each sister's face to her name. He wasn't having much luck, though, considering he'd been introduced to all of them almost at once. As for their husbands and children . . . well, the only one he could place was Jack Stone.

But then, one usually does remember one's rescuer.

"Luke, let Max get up on your lap," Camry said, leaning close to be heard over the sounds of lively conversation. "His feelings are hurt because I'm holding Tigger."

Well, why the hell not? He already looked ridiculous in his hat, why not try to hold an overly excited fifty-pound dog on his lap, too?

He turned his chair slightly, bumped into

someone and apologized, then patted his chest. "Come on, Max. You sit quietly, and I'll share my piece of cake with you after they blow out the candles." Max jumped up, then immediately tried to crawl onto the table, apparently more interested in the gift sitting next to Camry's cake than he was in the cake. "No, boy. Sit," Luke commanded.

Max sat still for exactly six seconds, then made another lunge for the gift.

In his scramble to catch him, Luke's chair again bumped into the person behind him, and with a muttered curse, both Luke and Max fell to the floor—the gift clamped in Max's mouth.

Camry looked down, obviously trying not to laugh. "Are you having a bad day, Luke?" she asked, a snicker escaping.

"You don't know the half of it, since you slept through most of it," he said, standing up. He then tried to wrestle the gift out of Max's mouth, painfully aware that there was sudden silence, and that every eye in the room was on him. "Come on," he hissed under his breath, "give it up, Max."

The dog opened his jaws without any warning, releasing his treasure. Luke was so surprised that he bumped into his chair—which finally sent the long-suffering person behind him scrambling away—then fumbled to catch the gift that went soaring through the air toward the table.

It landed directly on top of Camry's birthday cake with a *splat,* sending tiny missiles of icing over anyone unlucky enough to be sitting nearby. Leaving the gift in the cake and Max on the floor, Luke straightened his pointy hat and sat down.

The gift suddenly gave a long, air-piercing, cake-shuddering *beep.*

Camry gasped so loud it had to have hurt.

Luke merely closed his eyes with a groan. Oh yeah, miracles notwithstanding, he was having a very bad day.

"Did you hear that?" Camry said, nudging him hard enough to leave a bruise.

"Half of Pine Creek heard it," he muttered, opening his eyes just in time to catch Tigger when she shoved the dog at him and stood up.

"Mama!" she shouted down the table—though he didn't know why, since the room was filled with absolute silence. "What's in my gift?"

Grace shrugged. "I have no idea." She gestured toward all the other gifts sitting beside each of her daughters' individual birthday cakes. "Your gift was delivered this afternoon by special messenger. There was a card, addressed to me, that said I could tuck my gift to you away for next year, because you would probably prefer this one instead."

"But who is it from?"

Grace shrugged again. "The card didn't say."

"And ye just brought it into the house without knowing what was inside?" Grey asked, standing up—as did Jack Stone, Robbie MacBain, and several other men, including Luke. Greylen walked down and snatched the gift out of the cake. "My God, woman, ye should know better than that."

"It's okay, Grey," Grace said, also standing up. "Because I have a pretty good idea what it is. The card also said that twenty years was a long time for a woman to wait for her dream to come true, but that he guessed patience was a motherhood thing." She gestured toward the gift. "And after what Camry told us earlier, I now also have a good idea who it's from. That's why I went and got it from the shed just five minutes ago, and set it on the table."

Camry gasped so hard again that she bumped into Luke—just before she snatched the gift out of her father's hand. "It's the data bank!" she cried, ripping open the dark green paper that was covered with what Luke just now realized were long strings of equations written in gold ink.

She tossed the paper on the table, popped open the box, and pulled out a black metal box the size of a six-pack of soda. She held it up for Luke to see, then turned and held it up to her mother. "It's Podly's data bank, isn't it, Mama?"

Grace collapsed down in her chair, her face as pale as a ghost, huge tears sliding down her cheeks as her smile outshone the three blazing chandeliers over the table. "Y-yes," she whispered.

Camry ran up to her, set the data bank in Grace's hands, and hugged her mother fiercely. "We have it, Mama. We have your key to ion propulsion."

"N-no," Grace said shakily, handing it back to her. "You have *your* key." She touched Camry's cheek. "You unlocked the secret to ion propulsion when you were twelve, one day when you were in the lab working on a school project. You came up and looked over my shoulder and suggested I transpose two integers in the equation I was working on. So that makes it your discovery, baby, not mine."

Camry reared back in surprise. "But why didn't you shout it to the world? Mom! We could be traveling to Mars by now!"

Grace looked at Luke, then at her husband, then down at the data bank in her daughter's hand. "I didn't want what came with shouting it to the world," she whispered. She looked up at Camry, her face flushing red. "I know it looks as if I've been unselfish to let you be the one to present our discovery, but it's actually the opposite. I didn't tell anyone because it would have meant leaving Gù Brath for days or maybe weeks at a time, to oversee its implementation." She looked over at Greylen, her eyes filling with fresh tears. "So I very selfishly kept silent, refusing to let the world intrude on my *true* dream, which was spending every day at home with a husband and family I love more than anything else in the universe."

She swiped the tears running down her cheeks with the backs of her hands, then cupped Camry's face. "But you, daughter . . . you have a husband who not only will travel with you, but who will also keep you grounded—as mine did," she finished strongly, looking at Greylen again, her smile tender.

Greylen strode back up the length of the table, edged Camry out of the way, and pulled Grace into his arms, lifting her off her feet to bury his face in her neck.

Camry walked to Luke, her own eyes spilling tears. He handed Tigger to whoever was standing next to him, and pulled her into his arms.

The front door suddenly slammed, shaking the chandeliers. "I'm here!" a woman shouted. "You better not have started without me! Fiona threw up all over my birthday dress just as we were leaving, and I had to go back in and change," she continued, rushing into the dining room. "I swear she did it on purp—" She came to a sliding stop. "What did I miss?"

Apparently no one thought to answer her.

"What's wrong? Mama, are you *crying*?" she asked, rushing around the table toward her parents. She suddenly skidded to a halt beside Luke. She looked at Camry still in his embrace, then up at him. "Who are you?" she asked.

"If you're Winter, then I guess I'm your newest brother-in-law, Luke Renoir."

"My what!" She shifted the infant in her arms to free up one hand, which she used to pull Camry around to face her. "My what?" she repeated. "You're *married*?" She touched Camry's wet cheek, then swung toward the head of the table. "Why is everyone crying? What did I miss!"

The infant she was holding suddenly gave a loud wail and burst into tears.

"Oh, give her to me," Camry said, shoving the data bank at Luke so she could take the baby. "Go see Mom and Dad. They'll tell you what's going on."

As Winter bolted for the head of the table, Camry nudged Luke with her hip. "Come on, let's go into the living room where it's quiet. I have someone very special I want you to meet."

Luke followed her through the crowd of

whispering people, smiling sinisterly at Kate as she held up her cell phone and snapped his picture again on his way by, then stopped to gently close his mother's gaping mouth. He gave her a kiss on the cheek, then stayed leaning close. "You think this is amazing," he whispered, "you wait until you meet some of her *distant* relatives."

With a nod to André, he followed Camry out to the foyer, where he found her smiling up at a tall, handsome, rather . . . intense-looking man.

No worry he would mix up this brother-in-law with the others.

"This is Winter's husband, Matt Gregor. Matt, this is my husband, Luke Renoir."

Matt extended his hand. "Welcome to the family, Luke." His piercing golden eyes, glinting with amusement, darted to Camry as she walked away with his now-sniffling daughter, then returned to Luke—specifically to his hat—before leveling directly on him. "How is good old Roger?" he asked.

"As outrageous as I assume he always is."

Matt's grin broadened. "Yes, but he means well. So what did he con you and Cam out of?"

"Greylen's best snowcat."

Matt arched a brow. "Really? In exchange for what?"

"Marrying us." Luke glanced toward the living

room, then back at Matt. "And your enchanting daughter signed as our witness, along with your grandson, Thomas Gregor Smythe."

Matt also glanced toward the living room, then heaved a heavy sigh. "That girl is going to be the death of me," he muttered. He looked back at Luke, shaking his head. "You and Cam decide to have children, pray they're boys." He gestured toward the once-again-boisterous dining room. "I swear I don't know how Greylen survived raising seven daughters." With a shudder, apparently to shrug off his fatherly terror, Matt slapped Luke on the shoulder and nudged him toward the living room. "You better go save your wife from Fiona, before the little imp gives Cam the idea that she needs a baby of her own."

"Oh, and Luke?" Matt said just as Luke was about to enter the living room. "Thanks for keeping a close eye on my daughter last week."

"Trust me, it was my pleasure," Luke said with a nod.

When Matt nodded back, then turned and walked into the dining room, Luke went over and sat down beside Camry on the couch.

She immediately plopped Fiona on his lap. "Where's the data bank?" she asked.

Luke peered down at the large blue eyes peering up at him, and smiled. "I left it on the table," he said absently, gently bouncing his knee. "Hello there, Miss Fiona. Been doing much traveling lately? And have you decided yet what you want to be when you grow up?"

Fiona's answer was to pat her hands together—though she missed more times than she connected—and blow bubbles as well as produce cute little belly laughs.

"She's going to be a rocket scientist like her auntie Cam," Camry murmured, leaning on Luke's arm as she smoothed down Fiona's soft blond hair. "Isn't she beautiful?" she whispered. She tilted her head back to look up at him. "Wouldn't you love to have a daughter just like her?"

Just as Matt had, Luke shuddered in terror.

Which made Fiona clap her hands together again with even louder belly laughs. But then the infant suddenly looked down at Luke's hand and touched the ring. Camry held her hand next to his, and the baby awkwardly went after her ring.

"They're really lovely, Fiona," Camry whispered. "And every time we look at them, we'll think of you."

"Five minutes to solstice!" someone shouted from the dining room. "Cam, get in here. Mom's lighting the candles!"

Still leaning heavily on Luke's arm, Camry tilted her head again to smile at him. "I guess that means you pulled off your miracle, Dr. Renoir, and we're legally married. Forever and ever."

He kissed the tip of her upturned nose. "Uncompromisingly, unpretentiously, and unconditionally, Dr. MacKeage-Renoir. Forever and ever."

She melted against him with a sigh. "Thanks to this little girl," she said, leaning forward to kiss Fiona's rosy plump cheek. She suddenly stood up. "Come on then," she said, heading out of the room. "I don't care if my birthday cake is ruined, I intend to eat every last crumb." She glanced at him from the door, her eyes sparkling. "I figure the sugar should kick in about an hour from now. Vroom-vroom, husband," she purred as she disappeared into the foyer.

Luke immediately covered Fiona's ears with his hands. "You didn't hear that!" He hugged her to him with a sigh. "Thank you," he whispered.

He finally stood up and held her facing him. "So, Miss Imp, when do you think I should tell Camry not to waste her time deciphering the data in Podly's data bank?"

The sweet little cherub closed one of her beautiful blue eyes in a wink.

"I thought so," he chortled, tucking her against him and heading after his wife. "So it *is* on the wrapping paper you gave Roger!"